# THE FORTUNES OF TEXAS

*Follow the lives and loves of a complex family with a rich history and deep ties in the Lone Star State*

FORTUNE'S FAMILY SECRETS

With Archibald Fortune's death comes the revelation of a stunning secret: The Emerald Ridge scion had three separate families and one child he'd always longed to find! Can his shocked children come together to find Archibald's missing heir and claim the family inheritance—or will strife tear them apart?

*FORTUNE'S SECRET SON*

Hayes Fortune's world was already rocked by the discovery that his father had had *two* other secret families. But the revelation that Hayes himself is a father turns his universe completely upside down! Now he's determined to show Flora Rodriguez that he can build a life with his son...and with her.

Dear Reader,

I normally write books in the Montana Mavericks series, so when I got the offer to come hang out with the Fortunes of Texas, I jumped right into the mix. And let me tell you something, these Fortunes have given me a lot of backstory to work with!

Let me catch you up to speed. Hayes Fortune just found out that his father—Archibald Fortune—wasn't only married to his mom, he was married to two other women at the same time. And now Hayes has to work with his newly discovered half-siblings to fulfill the terms of his late father's will. Just when he thought he couldn't take any more surprises, he walks into Flora Rodriguez's shop and learns that he has a son of his own.

I can't wait for readers to fall in love with this new branch of the Fortune family tree and the fictional town of Emerald Ridge, Texas.

For more information on my other Special Edition books, visit my website at christyjeffries.com, or chat with me on X at @ChristyJeffries. You can also find me on Facebook facebook.com/authorchristyjeffries and Instagram Instagram.com/christy_jeffries/. I'd love to hear from you.

Enjoy,

*Christy Jeffries*

# FORTUNE'S SECRET SON

CHRISTY JEFFRIES

Special thanks and acknowledgment are given to Christy Jeffries for her contribution to The Fortunes of Texas: Fortune's Family Secrets miniseries.

Recycling programs for this product may not exist in your area.

ISBN-13: 978-1-335-14333-4

Fortune's Secret Son



For questions and comments about the quality of this book, please contact us at CustomerService@Harlequin.com.

Harlequin Enterprises ULC
22 Adelaide St. West, 41st Floor
Toronto, Ontario M5H 4E3, Canada
www.Harlequin.com

HarperCollins Publishers
Macken House, 39/40 Mayor Street Upper,
Dublin 1, D01 C9W8, Ireland
www.HarperCollins.com

**Printed in Lithuania**

**Christy Jeffries** graduated from the University of California, Irvine, with a degree in criminology and received her Juris Doctor from California Western School of Law. But drafting court documents and working in law enforcement was merely an apprenticeship for her current career in the dynamic field of mommyhood and romance writing. Christy lives in Southern California with her patient husband, two sarcastic sons and a sweet husky who sheds appreciation all over her car and house.

**Books by Christy Jeffries**

***Fortunes of Texas: Fortune's Family Secrets***

*Fortune's Secret Son*

***Montana Mavericks: The Tenacity Social Club***

*Their Maverick Summer*

***Montana Mavericks: The Anniversary Gift***

*Sweet-Talkin' Maverick*

**Harlequin Special Edition**

***Montana Mavericks: Lassoing Love***

*The Maverick's Holiday Delivery*

***Furever Yours***

*It Started with a Pregnancy*
*It Started with a Puppy*

***Montana Mavericks: What Happened to Beatrix***

*His Christmas Cinderella*

Visit the Author Profile page
at Harlequin.com for more titles.

To Phaedra McMahan, who often gets mistaken for being my sister since we look so much alike. School PTO meetings, Jazzercise, and dirty sodas on road trips are always so much more fun when you're there. You're the first one to ask me about my latest release and usually the only one to catch some of those hidden details in my books. I am so honored to be a "sister friend" with you.

# Chapter One

The months Hayes Fortune spent in the hospital learning how to walk again were a breeze compared to the past two months following the reading of his deceased father's will. He took a deep breath of the crisp spring air as he exited the Coffee Connection in Emerald Ridge, Texas. When that didn't help lessen the growing frustration churning in his gut, he ran a hand through his hair before shoving his favorite Stetson back on his head.

Hayes had always considered himself to be a guy's guy. He played high school football, drank his first beer before he was old enough to grow a full beard, busted some of the wildest broncs in the pro rodeo circuit, and smoked a mean brisket. If something involved frills, drama or anything remotely girly, Hayes wanted nothing to do with it.

That was why he was astounded to realize that the only people making sense in his life right now were the three women his father's attorneys recently informed him were actually Hayes's half sisters. Yep. Three half sisters he'd never known about, plus a potential fourth half-sibling out there somewhere, all sharing a father who'd left them a legacy of tangled lies and secrets they now had to unravel.

Things like this weren't supposed to happen in real life. How could a man have three separate families and manage to keep everyone from finding out about it? It was unheard-of. Even the old, cynical private investigator Hayes hired had been in awe when he'd learned the details of the case. And that guy had seen some crazy stuff in his thirty-year career as a retired Texas Ranger.

Hayes paused at the crosswalk to check his cell phone and saw an email from his former boot sponsor and two missed calls from his Realtor who was trying to negotiate a deal on a piece of property in Montana—the perfect spot for expanding his free rodeo camps outside of Texas. Unfortunately, there was still no response from his brother, Penn.

It would sure be nice if Penn, the one sibling Hayes had actually grown up with, would put aside whatever had him so worked up and join the rest of the family for the greater good.

Shoving his phone into his back pocket, he muttered a curse word that his mother wouldn't approve of him calling his brother. Then he waited for a sleek, extended-cab truck with shiny new wheels to pass before crossing the street. The town of Emerald Ridge was full of vehicles just like that one. Trucks made for ranch work yet driven by wealthy folks who liked to play at being cowboys and cowgirls. Not that Hayes himself hadn't grown up surrounded by the privilege of his father's wealth. It was just that he'd also chosen a profession that brought him back down to the reality of how many people weren't as fortunate.

Sure, some of the shops on Emerald Ridge Boulevard, like the feed and grain supply and the hardware store, catered to the townspeople who worked hard for a living and drove trucks with actual mud on the fenders. But some of the newer establishments seemed a little too upscale for anyone who wasn't living paycheck to paycheck.

Like that fancy French restaurant on the corner or this place he was passing with the children's clothes and toys in a window display that looked like it belonged in one of those high-end department stores in New York City. What was this shop even called?

His eyes scanned the storefront and landed on a sign that read Lone Star Little Ones.

No.

That couldn't be right.

Back in Houston, there was a children's clothing boutique with the exact same name. Not that Hayes had ever been inside it. He'd maybe done an online search of the company a year and a half ago, after spending an amazing whirlwind weekend with a woman who had seemed totally perfect at first. A woman who had the same Texas-shaped luggage tag on her carry-on that he had on his. A woman who'd offered to share her plate of buffalo wings with him after the hotel bartender told him the kitchen had already closed for the night. A woman who was so easy to talk to and laugh with that Hayes didn't mind a bit when the desk clerk apologized for not finding his room resevration.

Hayes nearly chuckled to himself at the memory…and the bullet he'd once dodged. His own mother had probably thought his dad was perfect at first, too. Yet, look at how *that* had turned out.

Still. That unsettled feeling he'd had since arriving in Emerald Ridge began to spread from his stomach to his chest. Surely, this wasn't the same store. It had to be some sort of knockoff.

Nope, Hayes realized when he saw the logo: a silhouette of a toddler holding a lasso. He remembered thinking the brand was an odd way to memorialize a brother who'd died doing something his family so obviously deplored.

Don't overreact, he told his pounding heart. Maybe she was expanding her business with a second location. People did that all the time. It didn't mean she was actually here in Emerald Ridge. Although, Hayes knew it would bug him if he didn't find out for sure. He'd had enough surprises in the past few months and didn't need another one hanging over his head.

Just like the way he used to wrap the bronc rein around his palm before giving the gateman a firm nod, he took a deep breath then pulled open the door and stepped inside the shop.

His entire rodeo career had been built on the premise to always expect the unexpected. However, no amount of deep breaths or bronc busting could have prepared him for the biggest shock of his life.

Flora Rodriguez was holding her nine-month-old son, Mateo, who was modeling one of the new adorable spring onesies and soft denim jeans that had just come in. A pregnant shopper was asking about the onesie's environmentally sourced organic cotton while the woman's mother-in-law played peekaboo with Mateo.

When the bells above the door jangled, Flora heard her part-time sales associate call out a greeting, allowing her to focus on reassuring the soon-to-be mom that Lone Star Little Ones only sold the best quality products.

Shifting Mateo higher on her hip, Flora delivered what was beginning to sound like the store's latest slogan. "I wouldn't put my own baby in anything less."

"In that case—" the mother-in-law winked at Mateo "—we'll take one in each color and size."

As Flora turned to make her way to the sales counter, she realized that whoever had just entered the shop hadn't made it past the first table display of miniature-sized boots and denim jackets.

When her eyes finally landed on the stone-cold face under the brim of the black Stetson, she gasped.

Hayes Fortune.

The man hadn't said a word yet and Flora couldn't tell if he was either frozen in place from the shock, or if he was politely remaining silent until she finished with her customers. When Mateo tried to lunge forward with his arms outstretched toward Hayes, Flora realized that maybe *she* was the one frozen in place.

Clearing her throat, she gave the two women what she hoped looked like a carefree smile and said, "Sue will ring you up."

"I'll do what?" the sales associate asked, her eyes wide behind her blue-framed glasses. Sue was a retired preschool teacher and godsend of an employee when it came to creating window displays and rocking Mateo to sleep in the back storeroom when Flora had him at the shop past nap time. But she had yet to master the computerized register. In fact, the older woman had once left a full shopping cart in the middle of the ER Grocery when she found out they'd installed a self-checkout lane.

But Flora couldn't worry about a potential five-figure sale or Sue breaking another handheld scanner. The only thing she could think about was the way Hayes was staring intently at her son and the way her throat was throbbing.

"What are you doing in Emerald Ridge?" she finally managed to ask.

"Apparently, I'm finding more long-lost relatives." Except Hayes wasn't looking at Flora when he said the words. His gaze remained steadily focused on the identical blue eyes of Mateo Hayes Rodriguez. The only visible concession to Mateo's Mexican-American heritage was that he'd inherited his mother's dark hair and tan skin. Otherwise, the nine-month-old was almost the spitting image of his father.

Flora shook her head to clear it. He'd said *relatives*. Plural. That meant he wasn't only talking about Mateo.

Admittedly, during their passion-filled weekend together, she had spent more time tracing the outline of his muscled abdomen than tracing his family lineage. When she'd first decided to move to her parents' vacation home in Emerald Ridge, she'd heard that there were Fortunes in town. But there were Fortunes all over Texas. That's why she'd made discreet inquiries to ensure the ones who lived here weren't related to anyone named Hayes.

She hadn't realized she'd said the last part aloud until she heard whispering coming from the sales counter and remembered that they weren't alone in the store.

"Yeah, well up until a few months ago, you would've been right," Hayes said, sounding just as mysterious as he'd been when she'd met him eighteen months ago. He tipped his hat in acknowledgment toward the two women who were openly staring at them. Fortunately, the only thing Sue was gaping at was the computer screen that kept buzzing in error every time she tapped the keyboard.

"Would you excuse me for just a minute?" Flora said to Hayes. She'd tried not to allow herself to envision what it would be like if he ever found out about Mateo. But if she had, it wouldn't have been inside her children's clothing store with Sue mumbling four-letter words about technology while customers watched the drama unfold. Before he could answer, Flora added, "Don't leave yet."

"It wasn't me who left the first time, Flora." Hayes's tense smile was more of a grimace, his unspoken accusation hanging in the air between them. "But don't worry. Wild horses couldn't drag me away."

"Here, Sue." Flora walked quickly to the register area. "If you want to take this little guy to the storeroom for his bottle, I'll finish up with these ladies."

Her employee had never looked so relieved to have a task that better suited her. She gladly hoisted the baby into her arms and went through the swinging saloon doors to the back. Flora tried to keep her fingers from trembling as she finished the sale and wrapped outfit sets in tissue paper before placing them in the butter-yellow canvas shopping bags that Lone Star Little Ones was known for. But she could feel Hayes watching her from the display shelf of children books along the side wall, where he'd posted himself.

As soon as the customers left and the two of them were finally alone, she suddenly wished she had taken longer ringing up the sale. Not that she was afraid of the tall, commanding man she'd once shared a bed with. The man who'd given cute little nicknames to the two matching freckles on her inner…

Again, Flora had to shake her head as though she could clear away the intimate memory. Then she used the rubber band she handily kept on her wrist to gather her hair back, as though she could also pull all of her runaway thoughts into some tidy semblance of order.

Hayes took several steps toward her and Flora decided that it was best if she met him halfway. Or at least didn't appear to be hiding behind the sales counter. She opened her mouth to explain what had happened. To make him understand why she hadn't reached out to him over a year ago when she'd first seen those two lines on the pregnancy test. But no words came out.

It was Hayes who finally said the quiet part out loud. "I don't even have to ask, Flora. I can see that he's my child."

A cry came from the storeroom area and both of them immediately turned in that direction.

"Do you need to go get him?" he asked.

Mateo had always been an easygoing baby, thank goodness, and rarely didn't do more than fuss when he was hungry or needed a diaper change. It wasn't like him to cry nonstop like this, especially as loudly as he was now. Not wanting Hayes to think there was something she couldn't handle, Flora pivoted to go check on him just as Sue came out with a very distraught Mateo who was twisting and wiggling in her arms.

"I've never seen him this way," Sue protested over his wails. "I'm not sure what's wrong—"

"Whoa," Hayes said loudly just before Mateo pitched his body backward. Flora raced forward, but it was Hayes's large hand on Mateo's back that prevented the fall. "The kid moves fast."

Flora was thinking the same thing about her son's father, considering she hadn't even seen him move toward them. Yet the man had gotten there before her.

It was either the near fall or suddenly hearing the unfamiliar male voice that startled Mateo enough to pause his crying. The baby's wet lashes blinked as he stared up at Hayes.

"Okay, big boy," Sue said before passing Mateo to Flora. "Ol' Sue's had enough excitement for one morning. I'm going to walk on over to Coffee Connection to get a double espresso before your mama puts me behind that register again."

Mateo didn't bother with his latest trick of waving bye-bye when Sue exited the store. He was too busy staring at Hayes, who was also staring right back at him. Mateo extended a chubby hand toward the black cowboy hat and Flora took a step back so he couldn't reach it.

Mateo, with his tear-streaked face, made a lunge for Hayes. This time, the man caught and easily hauled the baby into his arms.

Flora gasped slightly, her now-empty hands remaining in midair as though she was prepared to snatch back her baby if need be.

"Don't worry," Hayes said. "I'm not going to kidnap him."

Mateo had the nerve to giggle at that exact second, as if he hadn't been bawling his eyes out only a minute ago.

"You think that's funny, huh?" Hayes smiled at the boy who now had a firm grip on the cowboy hat and was yanking it. "Yeah, it's pretty hilarious that your mom's nervous about me running off with you. She's a worrier, that one."

Mateo giggled again.

Not wanting to be the subject of whatever joke was being shared between father and son, Flora finally spoke up. "I saw the surprised look in your eyes when you walked in here, Hayes. Obviously, you don't have a well-crafted kidnapping plan in place. Yet."

*"Yet?"* Hayes lifted his brows, which must've helped loosen his hat because Mateo was able to wrestle it free. "Is that why you never told me I had a son?"

She didn't want to insult the man. But she'd be lying if the idea of Mateo's biological father showing up to take him away from her hadn't crossed her mind before. The Rodriguez family was wealthy and could afford to hire the best attorneys if it came to a custody battle. However, she also knew how much money rodeo champions made when they took as many risks as Hayes Fortune had. No telling how much of those winnings he'd managed to save over the years.

She decided to stick with the same explanations she'd been telling herself ever since she'd seen her baby's heartbeat during that first ultrasound. "That weekend we were together, you told me that you didn't want children."

"I told you that I was *hesitant* to have children," Hayes clarified.

"Well, in that case, I was *hesitant* to find out that you might've felt trapped into having a kid."

"It wasn't a matter of me feeling like I was trapped." He scrunched his nose as his son put the felt brim of a very expensive, and from the looks of it, custom-fitted hat into his slobbery mouth. "That can't taste all that good, partner."

Something about hearing him call Mateo "partner"

caused a flutter in Flora's chest. She didn't know if that was a good or a bad thing. Part of her appreciated the affectionate way Hayes spoke to her son. But the other part? Well, it resented the fact that he likely had to use the endearment because he didn't have a clue what his son's name was. Although, she couldn't necessarily blame Hayes for that one.

"He's teething," she explained. "Everything goes into his mouth nowadays. Chewing on something helps soothe his gums."

"I know what teething is, Flora." Hayes's tone might've sounded more defensive if he wasn't still watching his son with candid fascination. Or rather watching *their* son.

It was going to take some time for Flora to adjust to referring to Mateo as *theirs*. The fluttering sensation sank to her stomach as she watched the two of them together. Hayes may be enthralled with the idea of being a dad today. But once reality sank in, he would likely change his mind. In which case, there was still a chance that Mateo would remain only hers.

Yet seeing the baby's reaction to his dad, the way he'd cried when Sue had him in the storeroom and the way he'd immediately stopped as soon as he'd seen Hayes, Flora was now faced with the fact that she couldn't deprive her son of a father simply because she didn't like the man.

Not that she had ever *disliked* Hayes. After all, she hadn't really spent enough time with him to form a definite opinion. It was the man's chosen profession that she didn't like. And the unnecessary risks that came with it. Then again, his job most likely came with a travel schedule that would allow her to continue raising Mateo on her own.

Flora steeled her spine and asked, "How long are you in town?"

"That's a good question." Hayes exhaled loudly and ran a hand through his brown, short-cropped hair. "How much time do you have?"

Hayes hadn't even had a chance to ask Flora what she'd named their baby when another customer came into Lone Star Little Ones. Whatever preconceived notions he might've had about holding his own child for the first time, he wouldn't have predicted it'd be in some random clothing store owned by a woman he barely knew. Even his own dad, who wasn't exactly the pinnacle of fatherhood, had been at the hospital when Hayes and his brother were each born. Their mom had the framed photos of them with a proud, smiling, Archibald Fortune to prove it.

"Maybe we should both be grateful that there aren't any cameras out to document this awkward situation," Hayes mumbled to the boy in his arms. They'd been left to wander around the shop, browsing what must be the latest trends in children's fashion—apparently there was a market for retro Johnny Cash concert tees in toddler size—while his son continued to chew on the Stetson that was now sporting a very large wet spot along the brim.

When the male customer decided he better call his wife on speakerphone to ask if he should get the bright pink overalls in a size four or a size six, Flora managed to make her way over to Hayes.

"If you want to speak privately, without any interruptions, then I can probably slip away for a walk as soon as Sue returns from her break." She spoke in a soft and low voice, the same way she had that night she'd asked him if he wanted to come to her room. With her dark, silky straight hair pulled up like that, her brown eyes appeared bigger, her pink-tinted lips looked fuller. How could it be that the woman was even more beautiful than he'd remembered?

"Sounds good," he said, completely unsure of what a walk would entail with a nine-month-old. Although, he'd seen a row of strollers parked in the back of the store and figured it couldn't be that hard.

Several minutes later, Hayes ignored the vibrating phone in his pocket as he struggled to snap his son into the complicated five-point harness of the most intricate stroller system he'd ever seen. The hefty price tag attached to the handle suggested that it was the best in the lineup and he had no problem paying top dollar since this would be the first thing he bought his child. But the baby refused to stay put and kept reaching to be picked up again.

He hauled the boy back into his arms and steered the empty stroller to the sales counter where Flora was handing over a shopping bag to the guy who was already on the phone with his wife again asking what errand he needed to do next. Sue walked into the store with a coffee drink just as the customer was leaving. The older woman's mouth dropped open when her blue-framed glasses landed on Hayes. "You're still here?"

"Sue, this is..." Flora paused for a few seconds, then cleared her throat. "This is a friend of mine from Houston. If you don't mind taking over here for a bit, we're going to take Mateo for a walk."

*Mateo.* His son's name was Mateo. Flora had named him after her brother who'd passed away.

"In one of the demo strollers?" Sue asked. "Matty hates that one."

Well, that explained why the child had resisted being buckled up. "I can just carry him," Hayes offered.

But Flora's dark eyes filled with concern. "It'll be better if I grab his small stroller from the storeroom."

Had she made the offer because she didn't want other people to see him carrying their child and make assumptions? He doubted her source of concern was his injury since he didn't limp or show any other outward signs unless he was tired or overexerted himself.

The orthopedic surgeon had told Hayes that his spine was doing better than expected, but his physical therapist warned him against lifting anything heavier than a small hay bale for another month or so. Mateo was definitely lighter than that, though, and Hayes wasn't quite ready to let go of him yet.

Of course, he also didn't want to upset his son's normal routine like his own father used to do. Archibald Fortune would often be gone for long stretches at a time, traveling for both work and what turned out to be *extracurricular* activities, only to return home and expect his wife and children to change their household schedule to accommodate him.

That's why when Flora reached for Mateo, Hayes stood by awkwardly, his arms already feeling empty as she effortlessly buckled their child into the stroller. He wasn't going to force himself into their world. At least not yet.

Mateo only protested when Flora attempted to return the cowboy hat to Hayes, who waved his hand and said, "I don't need it. Let him play with it."

It wasn't until he was holding open the door for them that he caught a reflection of his messy hair in the shop window. His mother often told him that it wouldn't kill him to go without a hat once in a while. Using his hand to smooth out his wayward cowlick, he muttered, "If only my mom was here right now to see this."

Flora heard him and tilted her head before asking, "To see what? That she has a grandson?"

"Well, that, too," he said quickly, not wanting to admit that he was thinking about his appearance during a moment like this. Hopefully, finding out she had a grandson would be a happier surprise for his mom than the ones she was still reeling from. "I suppose we'll need to figure out a good time for her to meet Mateo."

Flora's head remained tilted as she studied him, but now there was also a little crease between her dark eyebrows as though she was considering his suggestion. He shoved his hands into his pockets so he wouldn't be tempted to reach out and smooth away the line on her beautiful face.

Again, Hayes didn't want to push his own agenda on Flora, but, come on. There was no way he was going to keep his child a secret. Especially not after everything that had happened with his family the last few months. Not wanting to come across as too pushy, he added, "I hope you're okay with that."

"I guess that depends," Flora finally said. "How do you think your family is going to react to the news?"

"My mom will be thrilled. She loves kids. My brother will be shocked at first, but he'll come around." At least Hayes hoped Penn would accept it eventually. But who knew what was going through his brother's head right now? He'd told his half sisters the same thing this morning back at Coffee Connection. It was a reminder that his family no longer constituted only his mother and a single sibling. "To be honest, I'm not sure how the others will react. I don't really know them that well."

"Right. You made a comment back at the store about long-lost relatives." Flora began to push the stroller again as they headed down the avenue. "When we met, I thought you told me it was just you, a brother, and your parents. You never mentioned any cousins or anything."

"Have you seriously not heard the rumors around town about my dad?"

"I don't even know who your dad is, Hayes." Flora's pace remained the same, as though she could simply outrun any conversation that might be too uncomfortable. "When I moved here, I made a few discreet inquiries to make sure you didn't have any connection to the Emerald Ridge Fortunes. Otherwise, I've been too busy to keep up with the gossip grapevine unless it involves a new take-out restaurant or an upcoming baby shower."

One of the things that had originally drawn him to Flora the night they first met, besides her sexy legs and curve-hugging dress, was how easy it felt to be himself around her. She had this way of smiling at him that made him feel as though he could say anything on his mind.

Apparently, that once welcoming smile was now a distant memory.

"Then I won't waste your time with my family drama." Hayes matched her stride. She was several inches shorter than him, but she moved quickly and gracefully. "I'd much rather talk about baby showers, too. Did you have one after finding out that you were pregnant and deciding that you would keep our baby a secret from me."

An older woman about to pass them nearly stepped off the curb, her eyes round as she stared at them.

Flora finally slowed down long enough to make a shushing sound. She quietly added, "I didn't *decide* that I would keep Mateo a secret."

"Really? Because I don't recall receiving so much as a phone call or even a text telling me that I was going to be a father."

She stopped at the intersection and aimed the stroller toward the crosswalk. "I know this may seem hard to believe, Hayes, but I *was* planning to tell you. Eventually."

"Like before his high school graduation?"

Flora sighed loudly, as though she had any right to be annoyed by the situation. The light changed to green, and she stepped off the sidewalk to cross the street. "I knew you were focused on your career and I was focused on mine."

"Right. I remember you being overly focused on my job that last day right before you walked out." He didn't want to rehash the argument they'd had right before they'd parted and immediately regretted the words as soon as they were out of his mouth. "What I mean is that you told me you needed a break from all the extra hours you'd been putting in at work, but you didn't want to go into details. You wanted to keep things light. You wanted fun. And man, was it fun. So fun that I thought I could talk you into staying another week and watching me compete. As soon as you found out that the rodeo was my career, you completely shut down. In fact, I didn't even find out about your store until I was looking online and..."

He paused to help her lift the front tires of the stroller over the curb and onto the walkway leading toward the park.

"You looked me up?" Flora asked.

"I mean I might've done a quick name search because I was curious. Not because I was being creepy or anything."

"Don't worry. I didn't think you were a stalker." Flora tilted her head. "Or even remotely good at stalking. If so, you would've contacted me much sooner. It's not like I went into hiding or anything after I walked out of that hotel room."

"Well, I didn't go into hiding either." Hayes didn't want to bring up his profession again, but his name was pretty well-known on the rodeo circuit. Obviously, winning a national rodeo title wasn't the same thing as winning the Super Bowl. But ESPN had done that short feature on him during the event in Las Vegas a few months after they'd met. "You're telling me you didn't so much as google me?"

"Only to make sure you weren't related to the Fortunes who lived in Emerald Ridge."

Now might've been a good time to mention that, coincidentally, he just so happened to *be* related to those Fortunes after all. Normally, he played down his last name because he didn't want anyone seeing dollar signs when they looked at him. But it had been obvious that Flora came from money, as well. Her jewelry. Her designer handbag. The way the concierge at the hotel where they'd met in Dallas had gone out of his way to greet her by name and ensure that she had everything she needed in her penthouse suite.

Instead, he asked, "So you're new to Emerald Ridge?"

"New to living here full-time. My parents own a place near the river that they use throughout the year when they want to get away from city life. My goal has always been to open a second location of Lone Star Little Ones, and it just so happened that the building came up for lease the same week I found out I was pregnant." She narrowed her eyes at him. "Which also happened to be the same week you won the Triple Crown. By the way, it was a great photo of you holding the trophy in one arm and that blonde country singer in the other. So, yeah, I might've caught a glimpse of you online, as well."

"First of all, that wasn't a trophy. It was a cardboard check. And second of all, I barely knew that singer. My agent had worked out some sort of collaboration deal with a sponsor—"

Flora held up a palm. "You don't owe me any sort of explanation, Hayes."

"It kind of feels like I should at least explain why some blonde had her hands all over me while you were home, pregnant with our child."

A young woman pushing a similar stroller gasped, then shot Hayes a disapproving look.

"I didn't *know* she was pregnant," he tried to explain to the stranger, but instead of defending him, Flora shook her head and kept walking. When he caught up to her, he lowered his voice. "Maybe we shouldn't be having such a private conversation in such a public place."

"No, we probably shouldn't." At least she was agreeing with him. "But I'm not going to have this conversation in my place of business either. Which is where you showed up, unannounced. Completely out of the blue."

"I know what unannounced means, Flora. It's the opposite of announced. Which is what most people do for events such as marriages and births. Because they're kind of a big deal." Hayes scratched his forehead, then remembered where his hat had gone. He leaned forward to check on how the teething situation was going and saw his son fast asleep in the stroller, the black Stetson covering the lower half of his body like a blanket.

"He'll wake up if you take it from him," Flora warned, the challenge in her eyes suggesting that she could become a fierce mama bear when it came to protecting her son.

"I'm not going to take it from him," Hayes said, slightly enjoying her sudden spark of passion. "But it's the only one I brought with me, so I'll need you to direct me to a store where I can buy a new one."

"Brought with you? Does that mean that you're only staying in Emerald Ridge temporarily after all?"

He wasn't sure if the expression on her face was hope. But if she thought he was leaving anytime soon, he would need to set her straight.

Before he could, though, she stopped the stroller to face him. "Look, Hayes, I should have told you about Mateo before now. I had my reasons at the time and even now I still have reservations. We don't know each other well enough to speculate about how things might have been if I'd handled the situation differently." She hesitated for a brief moment before going on. "I know that probably isn't the apology you want to hear, but I wasn't exactly prepared for this moment. I think we're both going to need time to adjust to—" she gestured between the two of them and then made a big circle with her arm "—all of this."

She was right. This was going to be a huge change for not only him, but for her and Mateo, as well.

Hayes sucked in a deep breath and slowly exhaled. "Fortunately, I seem to have plenty of time on my hands."

## *Chapter Two*

Flora didn't blame Hayes for being upset or for doubting that she would have eventually told him about Mateo. But would anything have changed if she had? His career was too important to him and her peace of mind was too important to her. Their lives were simply too different.

"What do you mean you have nothing but time?" Flora looked around at the park that was getting more crowded now that school was out for the afternoon. "Don't you have a rodeo you need to be at? Or an angry horse that needs to throw you off it's back?"

"As a matter of fact, I don't. At least not for the foreseeable future."

Uh-oh. This was the exact scenario she'd tried so hard to avoid. "Please tell me that you're not giving up something you're so passionate about just because you suddenly found out that you have a son."

"Actually, I gave it up last year because I found out that if I do any more damage to my lower back, I'll never be able to walk again," he clipped out. "In fact, my doctors are surprised that I'm walking now."

Flora heard the words coming out of Hayes's mouth, but it took her brain a few seconds to process them. Thankfully, when it did finally click, there was an empty bench nearby. She sat in stunned silence, a loose grip on the corner of the stroller's handle. Honestly, she wasn't sure if it was the implication of what he'd just said, or if it was the earlier shock of Hayes's sudden reappearance, that was finally catching up to her.

"Five minutes ago, you were pushing this thing with the focus and determination of a person wanting to rush through an unpleasant conversation." Hayes took the opposite corner of the handle, preventing the stroller from angling toward a downhill slope. "So why do you suddenly look like you have a million questions to ask?"

Flora had been in such a hurry to steer Hayes out of the store and away from her place of business, she'd forgotten her sunglasses. But that wasn't the reason she was squinting up at him now. Although, she did wish there was something covering her eyes from expressing every emotion swirling inside her right now.

"Because you loved the rodeo," was the best response she could come up with. Unfortunately, her tone sounded almost accusatory.

"I still love the rodeo, Flora." Now he was the one sounding defensive. Or maybe it was frustration as he bent closer to examine the back wheels. "Is there some sort of emergency brake on this thing?"

Nodding, Flora reached forward and flipped the small red safety latch into the locked position.

Hayes stood up and gave the stroller a couple of pushes as though he needed to test out whether the brakes were adequate enough. His concern over their child's safety was touching and nearly made her rethink his previously expressed opinions about fatherhood.

However, he quickly quashed that hope when he said, "Anyway, it's not like I wanted to quit competing."

Or would have retired for anything less than reasons involving his physical health. He certainly wouldn't have left the circuit for emotional health reasons—namely *her* emotional health. She couldn't bring herself to ask if it had been an accident that had caused a career-ending injury. It would bring back too many painful memories of sitting in the stands, seeing her brother's lifeless body lying in the center of the arena as the fuming bull—

*No*. Flora wasn't ready to think about Hayes going through such a painful ordeal, let alone talk about it. She rubbed her eyes as though she could wipe away the image of her brother that had been burned into memory. Her throat felt raw when she whispered, "At least you were able to quit."

Before she knew it, Hayes was beside her on the bench, one arm wrapping around her shoulders. "I'm so sorry for sounding ungrateful, Flora. The first thing I thought of when I came out of surgery was your brother and every other rider who hadn't been as fortunate as me. Thinking about the ones who didn't survive a similar fall made me fight harder to walk again."

She wanted to lean into the comfort of his embrace, but it had been so long since she'd let a man hold her. Eighteen months, to be exact. And look at how that had turned out.

"I almost reached out to you," Hayes confessed.

"When?" She pulled away slightly, causing his hand to drop to her upper back.

"After a particularly grueling physical therapy session. I was pissed at the world and wanted to tell you that you'd been right. That the rodeo was too dangerous. That I should've listened to you."

"Why didn't you?" she asked hoarsely. She meant why hadn't he listened to her. But he must've thought she was asking why he hadn't reached out.

"Because I didn't want you to see me like that. The weekend we spent together had been one of the best times of my life. You didn't care about my last name and you had no idea how many titles I'd won. I was able to just be myself because everything with you had been easy. I didn't want to be a disappointment. Not after you'd been incredibly impressed by my..." Hayes peeked at the baby in the stroller before saying, "Physicality in the bedroom."

Flora's eyes went wide as heat raced up her neck and spread all the way up her face to her hairline. "You can't just say stuff like that."

"Why not?" Hayes asked with an innocent tone. "I made sure he was sleeping."

"Well, we're all wide-awake now," a voice said from the opposite side of the walking path, and Flora sank lower in her seat when she saw two older women sitting on another bench watching them. "Might as well keep telling us about the *physicality* part."

Thankfully, Hayes was blushing just as much as Flora was. His hand moved up to where the brim of his hat should've been—if he hadn't let Mateo keep it—and he said, "Sorry, ladies. I didn't see y'all sitting there."

"Oh, we just got here a couple of minutes ago," the second woman said. Flora recognized her from The Style Lounge, the hair salon where Sue got all the latest gossip. "What did we miss?"

Flora slipped low enough on the bench, she was nearly hidden by the stroller. Living in a small town like Emerald Ridge had its perks. But it was times like this when she missed living in a bigger city where most of the population didn't know her. She could avoid participating in the rumor mill all she wanted, but that didn't mean she wouldn't eventually become the subject of it.

Hayes must've quickly recovered from his initial embarrassment because his color returned to normal and his smile grew wider. His arm was still haphazardly around Flora, even though she'd slouched so low it couldn't possibly be comfortable for him.

Uh-oh. Flora didn't like the sudden gleam that came to his eyes.

"Well, let me see if I can catch everyone up to speed. I'm Hayes." He moved his free hand from his broad, muscular chest and extended it toward the top of her head, which was probably all that was visible to the women on the other side of the stroller. "This is Flora. And the little guy sleeping under the slobbery hat is our son, Mateo. He's nine months old, so he's teething."

"He looks just like you," one of the women gushed to Hayes.

Really? How could someone possibly tell who her baby looked like when his eyes were closed and half of his pudgy little face was squished against the cushioned strap where his head had settled after he'd fallen asleep?

"That's exactly what I thought the first moment I saw him," Hayes replied, and Flora forced herself to sit up straighter. She needed to be ready to make a speedy departure if the man started disclosing too much of their private business. Yet, Hayes took the opportunity to reposition his arm across her shoulders again almost as though he was staking some sort of claim. "You can't tell right now, obviously, but he has my blue eyes. Doesn't he, snookums?"

She had to resist the instinct to cringe. She'd told him that weekend they'd met how she hated pet names like that. Judging by his suddenly cheerful expression, he was clearly doing it on purpose to annoy her.

Dammit. His straight white teeth were even more perfect than she remembered.

"He does have your eyes, *orgulloso*." Flora blinked sweetly at him when she saw him realize that she'd called him proud in Spanish. "But let's hope he gets my smile. How long did you have to wear braces again?"

"Five very long years." He smirked at her before turning his full grin toward the women. "Let's just say that my homecoming date said I ruined our pictures because the camera flash didn't react well to all that metal in my mouth."

*There it was.* Finally, Flora caught a glimpse of the carefree and charming Hayes that had captured her heart the weekend they'd met. No. Not her heart. Her interest. Becoming a mother must be making her more sentimental if she thought her feelings for Hayes back then had been anything more than a passing desire.

She needed to get away from him before she did anything foolish. Again.

Retaking control of the situation, she abruptly stood and unlocked the stroller's brake. "I just realized that I didn't bring a bottle or the diaper bag. I better head back before he wakes up."

Flora wanted to suggest that he stay and continue chatting with the older ladies in the park. She needed some time to process the potential impact of Hayes coming back into her life and how it was going to change things. But he was already standing and telling the women to have a nice day.

When they were out of earshot, Flora sent him a pointed look.

"What?" he asked innocently.

"You purposely made it seem like we were one big happy family back there."

"So?"

"So, living in Emerald Ridge isn't like living in a big city, Hayes. People know me—at least know other people who know me. You can drive off today and never give anyone you just met another thought. But I have a life here now. I have a business. Do you have any idea how quickly news spreads?"

"Oh, I have a pretty good idea." His tone was slightly smug; his long strides easily matched her pace. "That's why I wanted to make it clear that I'm Mateo's father. I don't want anyone speculating about what my role is in his life."

"Your *role* in his life?" Flora didn't bother to keep the frustration from her voice. "I haven't even decided what that will be yet."

"Hold up," Hayes said, but she didn't slow down. His injury must not be bothering him much because he continued to speak as he effortlessly walked beside her. "*You* haven't decided what that will be? What about what *I* want? What about what *Mateo* wants?"

"He doesn't know what he wants," she shot back. "It's my job to do what's best for him."

"It should be both of our jobs, Flora. But I was never given the option." His words shook the fragile wall of defense she started building around her heart. It also stopped her in her tracks. He was right—she hadn't exactly given him a chance to prove whether or not he'd be a good father. But before she could concede as much, his next question stopped her in her tracks. "Did you even put my name on the birth certificate?"

She opened her mouth, then closed it. If he decided to establish paternity, it wasn't like he couldn't get a copy of the birth certificate himself. Flora took a deep breath then lifted her face to meet those piercing blue eyes. "His name is Mateo Hayes Rodriguez."

His jawline was hard and rigid, his nostrils flaring slightly as he slowly exhaled. "You gave him my name."

"Legally, I couldn't put you on the birth certificate without your consent. But I still wanted him to have a piece of you, other than your DNA."

His expression remained stone-still, making his emotions that much harder for her to gauge. But he gave a slight nod. "I want him to have as much of me as you'll allow."

*Allow.* That must mean he was willing to work with her. This time, she was the one nodding her head in response. "I know that you might not believe this yet, but I really was planning to tell you about him eventually."

"Does that mean you're not opposed to some sort of a shared custody agreement?"

A chill went down her spine, fear settling into her stomach. She'd yet to tell her parents who Mateo's father was, but just the thought of a formal custody agreement made her want to immediately call them to prepare for the worst. No, it was too soon. There was no sense in getting everyone all riled up yet.

She rocked back on her heels. "You mean like when he's older?"

"I don't see a need to wait. He seems to like me already. Maybe we could alternate days or something." Hayes glanced down at her feet. "Why do you look like you're ready to take off running?"

"I'm not going to skip town or anything," she said, both to Hayes and to her own restless legs. "It's just that I haven't missed a night with him since he was born."

"I know exactly how you feel considering I've missed the past 275 nights or so with him."

She checked his math in her head and was surprised his calculation was right. Her guilt at keeping the baby a secret battled with her anxiety over letting a man who was little more than a stranger into her child's life.

"Look, I can tell that even the thought of this is tearing you up inside." Hayes shoved his hands into his back pockets. "I'm not going to take him from you, Flora. I just want a chance to be his father."

"We don't need to rush into any long-term decisions today," she said, desperate to buy herself more time. "We can ease into things by spending time together."

He lifted one brow, and she immediately held up her palms. "Not romantically or anything. Just, you know, the three of us hanging out like we're doing now. It'll be a more organic and natural way for you to get to know your son."

"Why not?" Hayes chuckled, then rubbed the bridge of his nose. "After all, the last few months have basically been one long get-to-know-my-family session."

"Okay, that's the second or third time you've made a reference about that." Flora's chest tightened at the realization that Mateo might not be the only one. "Do you have another child you just found out about?"

"No, but apparently my dad had several."

Hayes had just been about to tell her the ugly truth behind his arrival in Emerald Ridge when her phone rang. Sue had somehow charged the wrong amount to a customer's credit card and couldn't figure out how to reverse the transaction.

That meant Flora needed to get back to the store.

"Do you and Mateo have plans for dinner?" he asked as they hurried across the boulevard. When she didn't answer right away, he decided not to give her enough time to come up with an excuse. "Kids like pizza, right? We could go to Donatello's."

"Not enough teeth yet for pizza, remember?" Flora pointed at the Stetson still covered in drool.

And that was why Hayes had been so quick to agree to this whole organic family plan she suggested. He had no idea what nine-month-olds ate…or even how to change a diaper. But he wasn't about to admit as much. "Okay, so we need to go to a restaurant where they serve soft food that doesn't require chewing. I know better than to suggest ice cream for dinner. Hey, what about Chuck's Chili Wagon right outside of town? That's mushy enough for him to eat, right?"

Flora covered her mouth, but not before a small giggle escaped. Hayes had a feeling she was laughing at him, but he didn't care. It reminded him of their passion-fueled, carefree weekend together—how neither of them had taken things too seriously. Well, not until that last explosive conversation right before she'd left the hotel room.

Suddenly, he wanted to make her smile again. Except he didn't get the opportunity because Sue was standing at the door of the shop waving her arms frantically.

"What time should I be here to pick you guys up?" Hayes called out right before Flora went inside.

"I'll let you know," she replied, then pushed the stroller through the store's entrance before he realized that she didn't have his number.

He glanced at the clock on his phone and decided he'd give her some time to deal with the waiting customer and would call the store later. In the meantime, he had several missed messages and voicemails of his own that he needed to handle.

Three phone calls, two emails, and one brand-new black Stetson later, Hayes was back in his hotel room and decided his brother had been avoiding coming to town long enough. After scrolling through his contacts list and finding the number next to the hotel building emoji, Hayes decided this was a conversation that should probably happen face-to-face. Or as close to that as possible.

He watched his own image on the video call screen until there was a connection beep followed by the appearance of his brother wearing aviator sunglasses and getting out of a Maserati. Instead of saying hello to Hayes right away, Penn handed a set of keys to a parking attendant and adjusted the white earpiece as his phone connected to Bluetooth. "Don't pressure me, Hayes. I told you that I'm not coming out there."

Smiling, he lifted a questioning brow. "Not even to meet your new baby nephew?"

"Dad's attorney didn't mention any of them being pregnant at the will reading." Penn stopped in front of a brass luggage cart and gave a room number to a bellhop before returning his attention to Hayes. "So, which one of them had a baby?"

"If you're referring to our new sisters, Shelby is actually pregnant, but none of them had a baby. Yet."

"You mean *your* new sisters," Penn replied, then greeted a doorman wearing the distinctive Fortune Resort uniform as he walked into a lobby. "I'm still processing everything."

"Yeah, if you could try to process things a little quicker..." Hayes replied impatiently, "I know that the rest of us being forced to fulfill Dad's final wishes would appreciate it. But that's not the reason why I called."

"Right. You said something about me having a nephew, which doesn't make any sense if none of my supposed siblings have given birth yet."

"I said none of our *sisters* had one," Hayes corrected, then shook his head at his brother's puzzled expression. "It's *my* baby, Penn. I have a son. You have a nephew."

Penn tapped his earpiece again, as though he hadn't heard correctly, then lifted his sunglasses and squinted at the screen. Hayes simply kept his gaze steady as realization finally dawned on his brother's face.

"Wait. Your whole life, you've said that you never wanted kids. That you didn't want to be like our father. So then how the hell did you end up with a baby?"

"You make it sound like one was mysteriously dropped into my arms, Penn." That, actually, wasn't that far from the truth. "But from what I can tell, the pregnancy happened in the usual way. Probably the labor and delivery part did, too, but to be honest, I forgot to ask. It was the part where I found out about him that wasn't exactly usual."

"When did you find out about him?" Penn asked.

"Today." Hayes gave a very abbreviated version of running into a woman from his past since phone calls with his busy brother tended to be rushed. "It was the last thing I expected. But I'm telling you, man, the second I saw Mateo, there was an instant connection. Like this surge of protectiveness came over me. I don't know what's going to happen as far as custody is concerned and whether or not his mom and I can reach some sort of agreement. But now that I know I have a child, I'm more determined than ever to not be like Archibald."

"I don't know what to say," Penn said. "I mean congratulations, obviously. But wow. I'm just kinda stunned."

"Yeah, I'm still in shock myself," Hayes admitted gruffly. "I don't know how many more bombshells I can take."

His brother was quiet for way too long. His eyes a little too appraising, as though he was expecting something else. There was a note of hesitation in Penn's voice when he finally asked, "What other bombshells have there been?"

"You mean other than the one about our father being married to multiple women at the same time and having at least three other children that nobody knew about? And that in order for all of his offspring to get our inheritance, we have to work together to track down his mistress from thirty years ago and yet another unknown sibling?"

"Right." Penn nodded. "Just making sure nothing else had happened since you went to Emerald Ridge to sort through that mess."

"You know..." Hayes leaned closer to the screen as if he was about to impart a little secret. "It would be a lot easier for the rest of us if you came here to help."

"It wouldn't be easier for *me*."

"I guess I'm not getting it, Penn." He lifted his gaze toward the ceiling. "Why are you so against fulfilling the terms of Dad's will? If anyone should be mad about the situation, it should be me. You and Dad always got along fine. Hell, you're the only one of us who has their pilot's license. You certainly had way more in common with him than I ever did."

Penn shrugged. "Maybe that's why it's taking me longer to come to terms with such a huge deception."

"You can still be pissed at Dad *while* you're helping us. I can assure you that I'm still plenty mad at the old man and what he put Mom through." He scowled. "And I'll probably continue holding this grudge long after the terms of the will are fulfilled. But one thing I'm not mad about is that I've been given an opportunity to meet three incredible women who I'm proud to say are my sisters. Is that why you're staying away? Because of them?"

"No, it's not the animosity toward Dad that's keeping me away. And it's certainly not because of any resentment or dislike toward our new siblings. As far as long-lost sisters go, I'm sure they're not the worst. Although, Mom said the third wife is real piece of work."

Hayes wasn't about to argue with anyone on that point.

Taffy Fortune didn't seem to get along with anyone, including her own daughter at times. She certainly wasn't mourning the loss of her late husband.

"Like I said," Penn continued, "I don't want to be rushed or forced into anything. Some secrets are better left hidden."

Sighing, Hayes angled his head. He was about to ask what that was supposed to mean, but his brother's eyes darted to something behind the screen and he said, "I have to go."

The video call disconnected, and Hayes was left wondering how long it would take Penn to realize that the sooner he dealt with things, the sooner they'd *all* be able to get on with their lives. And as far as he was concerned, it wasn't a matter of *if* his brother would come to Emerald Ridge. It was when.

Hopefully, learning that he was now an uncle would help speed things up. While it was true that Hayes had always been hesitant about fatherhood, Penn had once said that he never worried about having kids since he could be whatever kind of father he chose to be. Maybe it was time Hayes took his big brother's advice.

Assuming Flora would be willing to let him be a present dad. It was hard to tell since she'd been adamant after their brief fling that things would never work out between them. Maybe Hayes should've been more insistent. If he'd tried to stay in touch with her, would she have told him about Mateo sooner? Would he have been there when his son was born?

After his surgery—when Hayes was stuck in a hospital bed with nothing to do but think about what would've happened if he'd declined the judges offer of a reride or if he'd kept his bronc rein at three fingers—it was his mother who had told him that there was no point in reliving all of the things that had gone wrong leading up to his injury. He couldn't go back and change any of it. The only way to move forward was to stop dwelling on the past.

Hayes wasn't going to sit back and wait for Flora to reach out. He found the number to Lone Star Little Ones and dialed.

# *Chapter Three*

Flora had never been a natural in the kitchen. She could manage the basics, but nobody was going to mistake her for a professional chef. When she was in her early twenties and living alone in the city, it had been easier to eat out. But since becoming a mom, she'd been determined to make more of an effort when it came to home-cooked meals.

And she was getting better, especially at making baby food. But when Hayes had called her shop earlier with a few restaurant suggestions, Flora panicked. While several people had seen them together in the park already, she wasn't quite ready to go entirely public about who her baby's father was. So she'd suggested he come to her house. Then she'd panicked again when she realized that she might actually have to cook an entire meal for another grown-up.

Thankfully, he'd offered to bring takeout with him.

The entire drive home, Flora reminded herself that he was simply coming over to have dinner with her son… *their son*…and not with her. This wasn't a date and there was no reason for her to get dressed up or add a fresh coat of mascara. But when she'd been changing Mateo's diaper, she hadn't been quick enough, and a stream of baby pee had shot into the air and soaked the shoulder of her blouse.

"Oh, you think that was funny?" she said playfully to her son as he gurgled out a tiny laugh. "You think I'd know better, being a boy mom for the past nine months."

She quickly unbuttoned her linen shirt. Knowing she didn't have time for a shower, she grabbed a baby wipe to clean her shoulder as she carried Mateo through the bathroom between the nursery and her bedroom. Flora caught sight of herself in the vanity mirror, saw that the tail of her damp shirt was still hanging out of the back of her pants and dislodged it. Staring at herself a moment longer, she decided that it was time to retire the comfortable but highly unattractive nursing bra. Now that Mateo had started eating solid foods, he'd also transitioned to bottles before naps and bedtime.

The problem was that the sexier bras she'd worn before her pregnancy didn't quite fit the same anymore. Not that anyone was going to see her undergarments tonight.

"It's *not* a date," she told herself for the umpteenth time. To prove it, she pulled a nondescript charcoal crew-necked sweater over her head. Then realized the outfit was a bit dark with the black ponte pants she'd worn to work. She stripped those off and shimmied into a pair of prematernity white jeans that required a silent prayer and a sucked-in stomach before she could zip them all the way up.

"Hopefully, he's running a little late," Flora said to Mateo, who babbled happily in response as he sat next to the black Stetson on the floor of the walk-in closet.

The doorbell rang right on time, though, and she'd barely managed to run a brush through her hair before picking up Mateo—and his new favorite hat—and heading to the front door.

The baby let out a squeal and kicked his legs in excitement when he saw Hayes standing on the front porch. Thank goodness she hadn't been the only one who'd changed outfits. Although, the thin fabric of his chambray shirt did a better job enhancing the muscles underneath than the sturdy Carhartt T-shirt he'd been wearing earlier. Again, Mateo lunged toward his father, whose reflexes were just as quick as they'd been earlier today at the shop.

"Hey there, partner." Hayes hoisted him into one arm without dropping the takeout bag in his other hand. What did drop, though, was the Stetson Mateo had been sucking on all afternoon. The baby immediately let it go so that he could reach for the brand-new one on Hayes's head.

"I don't know what's gotten into him," Flora said as she picked up the discarded hat.

"I don't mind." The way Hayes smiled at their son made her heart squeeze tighter. "When I bought this one today, I asked the store to order an extra, as well. Just in case I need another backup."

"I didn't mean his fascination with this." She used the slobbery hat to gesture Hayes inside before closing the door. "Although, that's also a new phase apparently. I meant the way he just throws himself at you with no warning."

Hayes's smile turned into a slight smirk. "I seem to recall his mother doing the same thing the night we first met."

Flora legs suddenly felt wobbly, but she quickly took

the takeout bag from him before he could see the heat spread across her cheeks. There was no way she was going to fall for his flirtatious act again. She needed to get him to the least sexy room in the house. "Let's head to the kitchen."

"Lone Star Little Ones must be doing pretty well to afford a place in this neighborhood."

"If that's your way of trying to find out if I'm going to ask for child support, we can talk about that later."

"That wasn't my way to find out anything," he said from behind her as he followed. "But, yes, we can talk about child support later. And my intention to pay it."

She continued walking without so much as turning around, yet he easily caught up to her. When she finally paused at the entryway to the kitchen, which wasn't wide enough for both of them, he told her, "I hope you know, Flora, that I don't intend to be a deadbeat dad."

His steel-blue gaze was steady and determined and left no doubt about his sincerity. She shouldn't have been so accusatory a few seconds ago. Sighing, she responded to his earlier remark. "This is actually my parents' house. It was originally a vacation home that nobody ever seemed to find enough time to use. But once I decided to move to Emerald Ridge and open the second store, my folks have been coming out more often."

He glanced back at the formal living room that normally seemed huge to Flora—but now felt miniscule with a six-foot cowboy standing so close and filling up the space. "Then I'll likely be meeting them at some point soon."

"I don't know about that. They're currently out of the country with my sister," Flora answered, trying not to think about how fast her parents would be on the first flight back to the United States the minute they found out about this latest development. As excited as they'd been to welcome their first grandchild, the Rodriguezes had been less than thrilled when their normally easy-going daughter had put her foot down when it came to answering all of their questions. She continued toward the kitchen. "I'm sure you won't be in Emerald Ridge that long."

He chuckled behind her. "My mom said the exact same thing to me two months ago."

"You've been in town for two whole months, and we only ran into each other today?" She set the bag of food on the oversize kitchen island, then she dropped the drool-covered hat she'd been carrying on one of the counter stools. "Not that I get out much with the new store and, you know, having a nine-month-old. Still, it's a small enough town that I can't go to the grocery store without seeing at least one person I recognize."

"I stay at the Emerald Ridge Hotel when I'm in town, which is only sporadically. I've been back and forth a lot between here and my camps."

"What camps?"

"Saddle Up. It's a free youth program I started for kids who are interested in roping and riding."

"You mean you teach kids how to rodeo?" Flora hated the critical tone of her voice, but she couldn't help it.

"I give them the opportunity to learn about horses and ranching and other career options that they might not be exposed to in their urban neighborhoods. If they decide that they want to compete in events, then I want to teach them the safest way to do so."

"I hope you tell them that the safest way is to stay as far away from the rodeo arena as possible."

"Using that logic, the safest way to go through life is live in a padded bubble and only experience the real world by watching it pass you by on a screen. But you'll be glad to know that I don't minimize the risks either. Saddle Up campers get to experience every aspect of life on a working ranch, from shoveling horse dung to vaccinating calves to washing dishes in the bunkhouse kitchen. There's a lot more to rodeoing than the glory of winning a big ol' belt buckle and enough prize money to get you to the next competition."

"Then why in the world would anyone want to put themselves through it?"

"Do you really want to go down this road again?" he asked.

It was a *short* road. Or at least it was the last time they'd argued about it. That also happened to be the last time she'd seen him before today. Flora had told him that she'd already lost a brother to the dangerous sport and wasn't about to fall in love with someone who was so determined to take the same risks. They'd parted ways after that, her heart bruised but still intact. Now, however, she had a child with the man. A child who could also be hurt if he was encouraged to follow his father's risky career choices. "We can revisit that road later. Right now, I'd rather talk about why you're in town."

He ran a hand through his hair. Eighteen months ago, her fingers had done the same thing when he'd lowered his head below her waist—

Nope. That passion-filled weekend needed to stay in

the past where it belonged. She definitely wasn't going down *that* road again.

Mateo made a grunting sound and pointed a chubby finger toward the basket of fruit on the kitchen counter, reminding the adults that he was more interested in his next meal than he was in hearing their tense and awkward conversation.

"You can have some banana after you finish your peas," Flora told her son. Then turning to Hayes, asked, "Would you mind getting him in his high chair while I get his food? It'll be easier to feed him before we eat."

"No problem," he said. "I hope your high chair isn't as complicated as your stroller, partner."

As she moved to the refrigerator, Flora had to remind herself that she did this every day and Hayes was new to the world of baby gear and gadgets. Luckily, the high chair was wooden with a minimalistic design. If he could put saddles and bridles on horses, then it should be simple enough for him to figure out.

What *wasn't* so simple was the decision she faced as she stared at the options before her. As much as she wanted to show off her motherhood skills by bringing out the freshly made pea puree she'd learned to make from a mom influencer's video blog, Flora also risked her son throwing another fit if she tried to make him eat something he had so loudly rejected the night before. Mateo was an easy enough baby for the most part and even though Flora wasn't sure how long Hayes would want to play the role of father, she didn't want to be the reason the man took off running.

She decided to do exactly what she would've done tonight for dinner if Hayes wasn't there. She took the glass jar of smashed peas and filled a small copper pot with a couple of inches of hot water from the kettle faucet behind the range.

"I've never actually seen someone use one of those things," Hayes said from the other side of the enormous gourmet kitchen. "My dad insisted on having one of those things installed in our house when I was growing up. But he didn't spend that much time in the kitchen—or at home for that matter. And my mom refused to use it."

Flora suddenly wondered what Mateo's paternal grandparents were like and how they would react to their son having a baby with a woman he barely knew.

"My great-grandmother also refuses to use it when she visits from Mexico. She calls it *pretenciosa*," she said as she placed the glass jar in the shallow water, allowing the food inside to heat. "Tita actually refers to a lot of things in the kitchen as pretentious, including store-bought tortillas and microwaves. Although she has no problem watching her favorite reality dating shows on an enormous flat-screen television. Is your mom old-fashioned, too?"

"No, my mom is quite the opposite. Although, she also loves those dating shows where the contestants have to live together in a big house on a remote island. Her refusal to use the pot filler was because the contractors my dad hired to install it broke most of the tiles behind the stove. Tiles that she'd hand-painted herself."

Flora used a pair of tongs to remove the jar from the water. She didn't want the baby food too hot, so she used a soft spoon to scoop out a small amount so she could check the temperature. "Is your mom an artist?"

"She likes to call herself a student of art. She has a

degree in art history and sits on the boards of a few museums. She teaches some classes, but she doesn't believe in selling her own pieces or making money off her art. That might change soon, though. My father passed away a couple of months ago and, sadly, my mom's financial future is going to depend on a lot of things."

"Oh, Hayes." Flora set a small bowl of warm, green mush on the polished table near the high chair. She reached toward Hayes's shoulder, as though she could offer some sort of comforting pat, then quickly pulled her hand back. She'd once touched him in the most intimate ways, but things were different between them now. Instead, she said, "I'm so sorry to hear about your dad."

Completely oblivious to the sudden somberness in the room, Mateo dropped the replacement hat he'd been chewing and stretched his arm toward the bowl that was out of his reach. Instead of retrieving his discarded hat, Hayes left it on the floor and picked up the bowl.

"Mmm. Looks like smashed-up peas for dinner, partner." Giving the contents a stir, he couldn't hide the grimace on his face when he sat on the dining chair closest to his son.

"You don't have to feed—" Flora started to say.

"Yummy." Hayes's overenthusiastic use of the word would've been more convincing if he hadn't lifted a heaping spoonful to his nose, sniffed the green blob, and then promptly shuddered.

Mateo gurgled a laugh, his smile revealing two bottom teeth. Flora still melted at the sight of her son's happy smile, but seeing Hayes's facial expression soften with awe melted her from the inside out.

Hayes sniffed the baby-sized spoon again and shuddered more dramatically, making the baby giggle louder. Then he waved the spoon near their son's nose and this time Mateo did a full body wiggle, mimicking his father's shudder.

Hayes's laugh was deeper, which caused the baby to giggle more.

Flora felt heat unfurl low in her belly and knew she needed to get her hormones under control. Clearing her throat, she said, "It might be funny now, but I should warn you that he won't be laughing as soon as he tastes those peas."

Hayes brought the spoon toward himself and instead of sniffing, inserted the bite into his own mouth. Flora gasped in surprise, which only made Mateo laugh harder.

"Yummy," Hayes said again, but he was even less convincing than the first time. He dipped the spoon back into the bowl. "It could use a bit more hot sauce, but you try it and tell me what you think."

When he held the second bite up to Mateo, the baby opened his mouth and promptly took a bite. Flora made another gasping sound and Mateo laughed as some of the peas dribbled out. The game went on with father and son taking back-and-forth bites, although, she noticed that the spoon barely had anything on it whenever it was Hayes's turn.

"All gone!" he announced when the bowl was empty. "Time for bananas."

Flora had forgotten all about the requested banana as she'd stood there watching her baby swallow way more peas than he had last night. "It'll take me a minute to cut up the banana. But you can give him this in the meantime..."

She found a fresh spoon and grabbed the small sealed jar from where she'd stashed it behind the fruit bowl on the center island. When she handed both to Hayes, he read the label. "Chicken? Is it supposed to be dark brown? This looks worse than the peas."

"I can't figure out why, but he prefers store-bought food to the homemade stuff."

"I'm the same way, partner," Hayes told his son. "Your grandma accused me of preferring truck-stop diners and fast-food chains to her home cooking. She thinks that's why I loved being on the road so much during the rodeo season. But even I would've passed on this chicken pudding concoction."

True to his word, Hayes didn't so much as sniff the contents of the second course. But he didn't have to. Mateo gladly accepted bite after bite while Flora cut half a banana into pieces that were too small to become choking hazards. She used a damp paper towel to quickly wipe away the remnants of the first two courses of her son's meal from the high-chair tray before placing the tiny chunks of banana in front of him.

"He can manage these ones on his own," she told Hayes, who was still seated in front of Mateo. "Can I get you something to drink?"

"That would be great, but I don't want you to feel like you have to wait on me. You've had a long day, too. If anything, I should be fixing *you* a drink."

Her heart fluttered and not because his words were necessarily romantic. But because when was the last time someone had put her first in the evenings? It wasn't like she didn't have help when she needed it. When they were at the store, Sue was like having a second pair of hands.

And her parents' house cleaner came twice a week and would babysit occasionally. But at night, it was just Flora and Mateo. Even with so much help, being a single mom could get lonely.

Still…

That was no reason to let her guard down with Hayes or allow any fanciful notions to get in her head. She'd chosen to be a single mom and when Hayes likely grew tired of playing daddy, she'd remain a single mom.

"Except you don't know where we keep the wine opener." She smiled politely and turned toward the temperature-controlled, glass-fronted fridge built into the butler's pantry. If there ever was a day that called for a drink to help unwind, it was today. "Do you have a preference for red or white? Or do you need something stronger?"

"Normally, I like to pair my strained peas with a healthy shot of bourbon. But I brought Italian from that fancy restaurant inside the hotel. So red might go better with our dinner."

"I love Cucina," she said as she returned to the center island with a bottle of pinot noir from Leonetti Vineyards. "They do this great antipasto plate and their bread is divine."

"The maître d' told me that you would like it." Grinning, Hayes stood and went to the paper bag on the counter.

"You told the maître d' that you were having dinner with me?"

He studied her intently, his expression sobering. "We agreed that you weren't going to keep me a secret, remember?"

"I wouldn't call it a secret per se." She glanced at Mateo, who was watching them as he picked up another chunk of banana. "I just wasn't planning on making any grand announcements until we were more sure about…" She trailed off so she could focus on the wine cork that was resisting her attempts to loosen it.

"That I'm going to stick around?" Hayes gently took the bottle from her. His finger brushed against hers, sending an electrical current of awareness through her. "I thought I already made it clear that I'm not leaving, Flora."

"And I thought I made it clear that I'm not just going to share my baby with a complete stranger."

"A *complete stranger*?" The cork popped out of the bottle easily for him—the same way her son had taken bite after bite of peas for him. "I don't remember feeling like strangers when we made that baby."

A shiver raced through her spine at his soft-spoken memory. She turned toward the cupboards to get a pair of wineglasses, glad for the excuse to put some space between them.

"You know what I mean, Hayes." She stood in front of the open cabinet, making sure her fingers weren't trembling too much to pull down the crystal glasses. "Just because we *knew* each other physically doesn't mean we know each other well enough to raise a child together."

"Then the only option we have is to get better acquainted." His smooth voice was inches behind her… his body was so close yet somehow he managed not to touch her as he slowly reached around her to grab the glasses. "Which is what tonight is about."

If she took the smallest step back, she'd be pressed

against his chest. But before she could make a move, there was a loud smacking sound and then Mateo's happy babble.

They both turned to see that their son had used his hands to smear the remaining banana all over his high-chair tray and was currently rubbing the mixture into his soft brown curls.

"Actually, *that's* what tonight is about." Flora jerked her chin toward the baby. "You getting a front-row seat to the not-so-glamorous joys of parenting."

Before she could tell Hayes that it was probably time to call it a night, he already had one of his sleeves rolled up and was working on the other. "So do we wash him down here in the sink, or is there a bathtub close by?"

# Chapter Four

"I've never given anyone a bath before," Hayes told his son, who was splashing in the water that only filled about a third of the oversize tub. He spotted a very rumpled and very feminine blouse on the marble tile beside his knee. One that looked awfully similar to the one Flora had been wearing earlier today when he'd walked into her shop. "Although, your mama did try to talk me into trying out the one at our hotel—"

"He doesn't need to hear about that," Flora interrupted as she came into the bathroom for at least the tenth time. Not that he blamed her for wanting to check up on them. First, she'd needed to ensure the water temperature wasn't too hot and then she'd had to find the blue toy boat because the purple octopus that squirted water out of its mouth was clogged. Next, she had to show him several different bottles of baby products lining the tub rim and explain that a little bit of tear-free shampoo went a long way. *Oh, and the plastic cup works great for rinsing Mateo's hair, but don't let him play with it afterward because he'll try to drink the soapy water.*

"I found this on the floor between the vanity and the tub." Hayes handed her the scrap of fabric and was rewarded with seeing her cheeks flush with color. "But

I'm guessing you'd rather me use an actual bath towel to dry him off."

She responded by disappearing briefly and returning with a fluffy towel sewn in the shape of an elephant. "I set out his pajamas on the changing table in his room. There's a container of lotion there, too. Pro tip—put the diaper on him *before* the lotion. Holler of you need anything. I'm going to the kitchen to make him a bottle."

Hayes had worked with livestock his entire adult life and figured a wet baby couldn't be any more slippery than catching a birthed calf. And he was right initially. But as it turned out, wrestling steers was much easier than applying lotion to a squirming nine-month-old. Especially when he was limited by the small confines of the changing table rather than having an entire corral.

"How's it going on here?" Flora asked as she entered the nursery.

"Well, the diaper may or may not be on backward." Hayes strategically positioned both hands on a squirming Mateo while bringing his shoulder up to his face to wipe his damp brow. "I finally got his feet inside these blasted one-piece pajamas, but I'd like to have a word with the designer who thought it'd be a good idea to put a bunch of snaps on here that don't line up."

He heard Flora's soft chuckle behind him and wondered if she'd purposely laid out the most complicated outfit she could find as some sort of challenge. Or to somehow prove that he may have been successful with the strained peas, but he wasn't quite ready to tackle single fatherhood on his own yet.

When she moved beside him, though, and gently reached her hand between Hayes's two arms, he was too mesmerized staring at her profile that he couldn't pay attention as she showed him how to close the snaps. In fact, he'd get rid of every zipper in Mateo's closet if it meant he could be this close to her anytime they dressed their son.

When the final snap was done, she turned her face toward him, their mouths inches apart. The sharp intake of her breath made it clear that she was just as affected as he was by their proximity.

Mateo yawned loudly, his tiny chest rising and falling beneath his parents' hands before he stretched out his pajama-covered legs.

"Do you want to give him his bottle?" she asked, her voice low and soothing.

Hayes nodded, not sure if he should openly admit that he wanted the full bedtime experience. He didn't want her thinking that he was trying to take over or insert himself into their little family unit. She already seemed nervous enough that his sudden presence would somehow upend the life she'd created for her and their son.

The oversize upholstered chair near the crib rocked back and forth as he settled into it with his son in his arms. Flora handed him the prepared bottle and the baby immediately wrapped his little fingers around it and brought it to his mouth.

Then Mateo's eyes locked on to his; staring up at him with complete trust. If Hayes hadn't already fallen in love with his child the second he'd seen the boy, he would've been a complete goner by now. His rib cage grew tighter, as though it couldn't contain this swelling feeling inside his heart.

Flora said something about their dinner before the

nursery lights dimmed and the soft sound of classical music filled the room. But Hayes couldn't take his eyes off his son's.

Suddenly, all the stress from earlier that day fell away. Hayes didn't think about his father's will, the upcoming meeting with his camp managers or whether his brother would finally come to Emerald Ridge. There was nothing he could think about in that moment other than the tiny human in his arms and everything he wanted to give this child. Everything he wanted to *be* for his son.

Mateo's eyes closed and his small body relaxed, yet Hayes held the bottle in place long after the milk was gone. The already peaceful room grew even more calm, and he felt the weight of his own eyelids.

A loud burp sounded, but the baby didn't stir. Flora peeked her head into the room yet didn't make a sound. She pointed at the crib, then at the sleeping infant before gesturing toward the crib again. As gently as possible, he laid his son in the small bed. He hadn't tiptoed since he and Penn were young enough to sneak down the stairs on Christmas Eve in an effort to catch Santa Claus coming down the chimney. If Hayes hadn't been wearing his boots, he would've tiptoed at that exact moment. Thankfully, the area rug was as plush as it was colorful and muted the sounds of his steps as he left the room.

Flora was waiting for him at the door and quietly shut it behind him. He followed her down the short hallway that led to a sitting room of sorts. Although he hadn't been given a formal tour of the stately house, it appeared that Flora and Mateo had their own private wing that was bigger than most two-bedroom apartments. There was a small table with two chairs pushed up against a wall; however, it appeared to be doubling as a desk with an open laptop, several files and a notepad covering the surface.

As he scanned the room, Hayes noticed the coffee table in front of the sofa had been set with plates, napkins and the bottle of wine they'd opened in the kitchen.

"What if Mateo wakes up? Will we be able to hear him?" he whispered.

She held up a device the same size as a walkie-talkie showing a small black-and-white video of the room he'd just left. "The baby monitor is on."

"No wonder you didn't keep coming in to check on me the way you did when I was giving him a bath." Hayes meant the statement to come out as a joke, but he could see the defensiveness flash in her eyes.

"I wasn't checking on *you*. I was checking on my child." She offered Hayes a wineglass, then sat on the sofa. "He doesn't always fall asleep right away when someone other than me is doing his bedtime routine."

"Do you go out a lot in the evenings?" Now Hayes was the one who sounded defensive. Or even jealous. But it was the first time he'd realized that there might be another man in the picture—someone else who would be raising his child. "Or have…ah…guests sleep over?"

Flora took a sip of wine, then asked, "Do you really want to talk about each other's dating lives?"

"We can." He took the seat next to her on the sofa. "Although, mine's rather nonexistent at the time."

"You said your father passed away two months ago." She studied him over the rim of her glass. "Is that why you're in Emerald Ridge?"

"That's the simple answer."

“What’s the complicated one?”

Hayes sighed. “I haven’t told many people about this.”

“Not even the maître d’ at Cucina?” She opened the antipasto container. “You seemed so eager to share *our* personal business with him.”

“I think he might know more about this than some of the other townspeople, considering Huey, Louie and Dewey love to eat there.”

Quirking a brow, Flora transferred some of the meats and cheeses to his plate with a fork and knife. “Huey, Louie and Dewey?”

“That’s what I call my dad’s attorneys. They’re identical triplets.” He unwrapped the bread and placed it between them.

“Triplet attorneys is an interesting start to this story.” An olive toppled out of the container and landed on his plate. She must’ve remembered that he hated olives because she quickly moved it to hers.

“That was the first surprise after my dad’s death. We’d always known Carlton Inland as my dad’s personal attorney, so it was totally expected when he came to our family home to read my father’s will. Except instead of reading the will, which he explained would be done the following day in Emerald Ridge, he read us a letter my dad wrote. This was the exact same letter that was read at the exact same time to my father’s two other wives and their children.”

Flora paused with another olive halfway to her mouth. “So, your dad was married before he met your mom?”

“Archibald had not only been married before he met my mom—he’d also married another woman after my mom. You see, my dad had been married to all three of them. At the same time.”

The olive fell off her fork, but Flora didn't seem to notice. "You mean your father had *three* wives? Simultaneously? And none of them knew about the other?"

"We always thought that he just traveled a lot for business." Even two months after the truth had come out, Hayes could still feel the sting of betrayal. But he noticed that it was becoming easier to talk about. Or maybe it was being with Flora again that made it feel easier. "Our sisters thought the same thing about him whenever he'd leave their houses to come to ours."

"Wait. You have sisters? From these other wives?"

"Yes. Agatha is my dad's first wife. Her daughters are Shelby and Jillian. They grew up in Emerald Ridge."

"So then, you *are* related to the Fortunes here," she whispered. "Why didn't that show up during my online search?"

"Probably because my old man went to extreme lengths to keep any information about any of his families under wraps," Hayes said. "The rest of us didn't know either, so don't feel too badly."

Flora gulped from her wineglass. "Fair enough."

Hayes continued. "My mom, Damaris, is the second wife. She raised Penn and me in Houston. The third wife is from Dallas. Taffy's daughter is Madeline."

Flora seemed to be following along at the list of names but then shook her head. "So, none of you knew about each other until two months ago? That must've been *some* will reading!"

"I don't know what was more shocking when I showed up in Emerald Ridge. Meeting the sisters I never knew I had or finding out that there were two other men who looked exactly like my dad's attorney Carlton. You'd think it would be the sisters, but sixty-something-year-old identical triplets in matching suits was a little bit more than my brain could process at the time."

"And these triplets—" she paused to pour herself more wine "—they all worked for your dad?"

"Yep. All of them are attorneys, each assigned to one of my dad's three families. For some reason, I think my mom was more upset about Carlton never telling her he had two identical brothers. I guess she expected more honesty out of him than my dad. Or maybe it was easier for her to be upset at the messenger since he was still alive. I don't know..."

"In any event, I bet everyone was pretty shook up." Flora passed Hayes his own wineglass.

"You'd definitely win that bet—lots of tears and confusion, not to mention a ton of accusations. But then my father, through the triplet attorneys, dropped the biggest bombshell of all. His estate is evenly divided between his wives and children. But in order for any of us to get our inheritance, we have to work together to find his sixth child."

"Wait...there's *another* wife?"

"No. He never married this one's mom. Surprisingly. She left soon after finding out she was pregnant. At least, that's what the attorneys told us. I don't know if my father ever tried looking for them on his own. But apparently he thought the rest of us could somehow manage the task and set things right on his behalf."

"Wow. I'm trying to process how something like this happens. How did your mom not know that her husband had two other wives?"

"Probably the same way I never knew I had a son. Nobody told me."

Flora sat up straighter, her shoulders squared toward him. "I hardly think this is the same thing at all. I wasn't purposely lying to you or going out of my way to keep you from finding out."

Hayes quickly realized how unfair his comparison had been between the two situations, and a pang of guilt swept through him.

"I shouldn't have implied that you had the same intent or would've gone to the same lengths as him." Although, truthfully, he couldn't help but wonder what would have happened if he hadn't found out about Mateo on his own. "I meant it more as a defense of my mother. Maybe she should've known or asked more questions about why he was gone so often. But when you don't know something—or someone—even exists, how do you know that you were missing all the signs?"

"That's fair." Flora nodded slightly as though she understood his explanation. However, her grip on the stem of her glass suggested she wasn't quite convinced that Hayes hadn't meant to insult her. "Your father must've gone to great lengths, though, to keep all of you a secret from not only each other, but from friends or acquaintances that could inadvertently let something slip."

"He had offices across Texas, and apparently houses, as well. He would spend a week or two with us in Houston and then he'd go visit the next family in their city. It's a lot easier than it sounds when you have your own fleet of jets at your disposal."

"Fortune Air?" Flora said loud enough to wake up the baby. She quickly checked the monitor before continuing in a quieter, but equally intense tone. "You're the heir to one of the most prestigious airline companies and yet you decided hopping on the backs of bucking horses was a better way to earn a living?"

"You are really stuck on the rodeo thing still, aren't you?"

"And you're really stuck on not wanting talk about it being the thing that kept us apart," she retorted.

"I *do* want to talk about it. Eventually." He brought his glass with him as he finally sagged against the sofa cushions. "But today has been a lot—of new information to process. A lot of questions and emotions. I'm not saying I can't handle it, or that the two of us don't have a ton of things to figure out. Just that the thought of starting an argument with you right now fills me with more exhaustion than my brain can possibly handle. I don't want to say something I'll regret…or worse…something that could cost me a relationship with my son."

"Hayes." She pivoted her body to face him, drawing her knees up on the sofa so that her legs were folded in front of her. "I don't ever want you to feel like you can't communicate with me. I'll admit that I've got an advantage in this situation because I've had more time to consider what kind of mother I want to be and how things would work once you were in Mateo's life. But I don't have all the answers, and I certainly don't know what tomorrow will bring. If we're going to successfully co-parent our son together, we need to be able to let go of some things."

Was she talking about setting aside the good memories they'd shared that weekend they'd met? Or that one not-so-great moment—those five minutes before she'd walked out of the hotel room and hadn't turned back?

Her knees were so close to his elbow, it would've taken

no effort for him to lift his hand and slide his fingers along the crisp white denim covering the curve of her leg. But he couldn't very well say he was too exhausted to argue, yet not too tired to make a pass at her. Instead, he asked, "So what do you suggest we let go of first?"

"I want to say we should forget about any past hurt or disappointment. But I know we can't magically make it disappear."

"How about we put it to the side for a few days and only talk about the thing that matters most to us?" He shifted his glass to the hand closest to her so that he wouldn't be tempted to push a silky strand of dark hair behind her ear. "Tell me about Mateo. Was it a difficult pregnancy?"

"I was a little hormonal at times, so you missed out on that fun experience. But overall, it was fairly average, I'd say. A little bit of morning sickness in the beginning, a lot of ankle-swelling at the end." Smiling, she settled deeper into the sofa as she talked. "The second trimester was my favorite. I had this cute little belly bump and I loved all the stretchy maternity outfits that took over my wardrobe."

Hayes leaned forward to pick up his plate. "Did you do one of those ultrasound things where they tell you whether you're having a boy or a girl?"

"The doctor did the ultrasounds to check on the baby's development, but I wanted to wait to find out the gender. According to my mom, who turned into a walking medical website as soon as I told my parents, it was a textbook pregnancy. Every developmental stage happened according to schedule, and my water broke exactly on my due date."

“So then labor went smoothly?” he asked but Flora was already shaking her head.

“Nope.” She popped a chunk of mozzarella into her mouth before continuing. “One thing about owning a children’s shop is I meet a lot of mothers and every single one of them has their own story about giving birth. So I knew to expect the unexpected. But after my water broke, absolutely nothing happened. I didn’t have any contractions or dilation. In fact, I didn’t feel anything different at all.” She sighed. “I walked lap after lap around the delivery ward, and they gave me medicine to induce labor. Yet Mateo gave no sign of wanting to come out and meet the world.”

“I’ve never seen a baby born, but I’ve been in enough stables during birthing season to know that’s *not* a good sign.”

“Right. As glad as I was that I wasn’t shouting obscenities or screaming in pain like some of the other patients in the rooms near mine, I was also aware that our baby couldn’t go without amniotic fluid for much longer. When the doctor recommended a C-section, I was terrified. I’d never had so much as a cut requiring stitches, let alone undergone surgery. I told the doctor that I should probably go home and take a nap. My mom suggested I eat *aguachile*, because that had caused one of her cousins to go into labor. But my dad was the voice of reason. He reminded me that women have C-sections every day and that the doctor knew what she was doing. My mom was a little annoyed when I chose him to be my person in the operating room. But he was a total rock star.”

Hayes couldn’t stop the guilt that washed over him

in waves. Nor did he want to. "I should have been there to support you."

"And I should've given you the option." She reached out and touched his shoulder. "But tonight we're not talking about the things we need to let go of, remember?"

He nodded, the tension in his jaw easing as they continued talking about Mateo's first few months.

Hayes had switched to a bottle of water, but when she started telling him what was meant to be a funny story about accidentally ordering a lifetime supply of nursing pads, he poured her a third glass of wine to get his mind off the image of her breasts and the way they'd once felt in his cupped palms when they'd—

A noise sounded from the baby monitor and he nearly knocked over his plate as he jumped up to head into Mateo's room.

"The baby's fine," she assured him, grabbing Hayes's hand and pulling him back onto the sofa. "That was just the speaker switching off because the music had finished."

He sat on the edge of the cushion, unable to feel totally settled or at ease unless he checked on his son himself.

"I know exactly what you're thinking," Flora squeezed his fingers reassuringly. "No matter how many baby books you read or how many pediatricians your mom interviews, there is always this nagging doubt that you might do something wrong. That a tiny little human is completely dependent on you and the last thing you want to do is mess up."

He swallowed, not wanting to admit that Mateo wasn't the only one dependent on her right now. Not wanting to admit that holding her hand felt so damn good right now. So right. Instead, he asked, "How many pediatricians did your mom interview?"

"Eight," she replied, staring at their interlocked fingers as he stared at her.

Although, neither one of them really cared about pediatricians at that exact moment. That physical connection they'd experienced a year and a half ago was still there. At least it was for him. Hayes had begun to think he'd imagined it at the time or was viewing their weekend together through a lens of nostalgia.

Finally, he used his free hand to gently tilt Flora's chin up until her eyes met his. "I need you to know that I really want to do everything in my power to be the best co-parent possible for Mateo. But I also really want to kiss you right now, so—"

She pressed her lips to his, her mouth cutting off whatever it was he'd been about to say. He could honestly no longer remember. Then, his fingers slid along her jawline until his hand could cup the nape of her neck before angling her head to deepen the kiss. Flora moaned and Hayes's tongue took advantage of the opportunity to explore further.

Taking the hand she was still holding, she brought his palm to one of her breasts and desire shot through him as he felt her nipple tighten beneath his thumb. He thought she'd moaned again, but it very well could have been him. This was exactly how it had been the first night they'd met—the second they'd touched, passion had completely taken over and all logic and reason had disappeared.

She must've made a similar realization at the exact moment he did because they broke the kiss at the same time. Although she created more distance by jumping to her feet first.

If her chest wasn't expanding and contracting with each panted breath, Hayes wouldn't have been able to tell that she'd been as affected by the heated exchange as he'd been.

He stood, as well. "I should probably get going…" Both paused, but when neither one spoke for another moment, he finally added, "Thank you for letting me be a part of the bedtime routine."

"And thank *you* for bringing dinner," Flora replied, but couldn't seem to meet his gaze. She was already stacking plates and clearing the table, the pasta entrées still in the containers since they'd barely made it through the bread and salad course before things had gotten physical. "Do you want to take any of the food back to the hotel?"

Hayes patted his stomach. "That's okay. I already filled up on peas."

Truthfully, he was still hungry. Not only for dinner, but for Flora, as well. However, if he wanted to be invited back to her place to spend time with his son, he should probably get out of there before they did something neither one of them was ready for. His first priority in Emerald Ridge was getting to know his son. His second was dealing with the mess his father had left. That meant getting Flora back into bed should be the least of his concerns right now.

Unfortunately, it was all he could think about on the drive back to his hotel.

# *Chapter Five*

"Who was here last night?" Regina, her parents' house cleaner, asked as soon as Flora walked into the kitchen the following morning with Mateo.

"What makes you think someone was here?" she responded, even though the eagle-eyed woman who'd worked for the Rodriguezes the past fifteen years knew the family better than anyone else.

"There are two wineglasses in the dishwasher." Regina held open her arms to Mateo, who gladly transferred to her. "Last time I checked, nine-month-olds don't drink wine."

And last time *Flora* checked, she was a grown adult who was allowed to have guests over. Although, there was no way she'd say that to the woman who'd once driven her to the mall to buy a replacement pair of stilettos when she had broken the heel of her mom's favorite shoes after being told in no uncertain terms that she wasn't allowed to wear them to her best friend's *quince*.

"I ran into an old friend at the store yesterday." She spoke into the refrigerator, pretending to be actively searching for Mateo's breakfast so Regina wouldn't see the flush on her cheeks. "They brought dinner."

"I saw that, as well." Her housekeeper reached around

Flora to grab a jar of preblended rice cereal. "I recognized the takeout boxes from Cucina that were barely touched."

"Thanks for the reminder," she muttered, pretending not to hear the implied question. "We're getting a new shipment of kid's swimwear today and Sue is going to need help getting the spring break display up. I won't have time to leave the shop for lunch."

"So then I guess we're not going to talk about your walk in the park yesterday, Matty," Regina cooed to the baby as she situated him into the high chair. She always did that—pretended like she was speaking to Mateo when she was really addressing Flora. "Or the handsome cowboy who was telling people that he's your father."

*Busted.*

Flora squeezed her eyes shut. When she opened them, the house cleaner was staring at her, one brow arched.

"How did you find out so soon, Regina?"

"My sister works at The Style Lounge. Need I say more?"

"I'd actually appreciate it if you could say *less*. Especially to my parents if you talk to them before I get a chance."

"Then I'd suggest you tell them soon, Miss Flora. The landscaper that works next door told me Mr. Paul already asked him if he knows anyone who drives a blue pickup truck because he saw one parked over here last night when he took Velvet out for his nighttime business."

Flora huffed out a breath. The River Estates HOA was full of busybodies who kept track of whose lawn was a quarter inch over regulation and who used Midseason

Mist paint on their window eaves instead of the already approved Agreeable Gray.

"I hope he told Mr. Paul that there are lots of people who have blue trucks. This is Texas after all."

"What he *should* tell Mr. Paul is his fluffy little dog keeps pooping on your front lawn," Regina replied. "But my point is that people are talking and if you have something to hide, you're going to need to do a better job of it."

"Nobody has anything to hide," Flora said a bit defensively, causing Mateo to stare at her with wide eyes. She softened her tone. "It's just a complicated situation and there are way more questions than answers right now."

"Then let me add another question to the mix." Regina used the corner of the baby's bib to wipe his mouth. "Is it true that the man claiming to be Mateo's father is also one of those supposedly secret children of Archibald Fortune?"

"Did that come up at the salon, too?" Flora was still reeling from the shocking story Hayes had told her last night. But as much as she wanted to know more about his family background, it felt rather icky gossiping about such a personal topic with someone else. Or maybe the icky feeling was from the green smoothie Regina insisted on making her two days a week.

"No." The older woman opened a small jar of pureed peaches. "My other sister works at the Emerald Ridge Hotel and told me about it." Flora rolled her eyes but didn't comment. She knew that while Regina might hear plenty of rumors from her network of sources, the woman was a vault when it came to oversharing anything about the Rodriguez family. Regina had been the one to drive Flora and Adrienne to the hospital when Manny died.

She'd also ironed Manny's suit and then carefully delivered it to the funeral home, staying to make sure the oldest Rodriguez brother was buried in his favorite boots. When it came down to it, Regina knew way more about them than any of the staff who worked at their home in Houston or at Rodriguez Oil.

So, when Regina repeated her earlier question about Mateo's father's identity, Flora heard herself admitting the truth for the first time. "Yes, Hayes Fortune is Mateo's father. I met him eighteen months ago when we were both in Dallas for work. It was a brief…uh…*situation* and we didn't really get into too many details about each other's backgrounds."

"Sounds like the apple didn't fall far from the tree, then." Regina made a tsking sound. "His old man apparently had the same habit of getting women in the family way. I heard they had to hire a private investigator to find Archibald's mistress and another missing sibling. Luckily, you were able to track down this Hayes character and now you're making him do right by his son."

"Actually…" Flora shook her head, unable to allow anyone to think the worst of Hayes. "I didn't track Hayes down. I could've as soon as I found out I was pregnant. And maybe I should've, at least that's what he thinks. But I didn't. It was completely by chance that he showed up yesterday at Lone Star Little Ones and saw Mateo."

"Wait a minute." The older woman had turned in her seat, the creases around her eyes deepening as she studied Flora. "You mean to tell me that you never even told this man he was going to be a daddy? He just walked into your store yesterday *and surprise*, he finds out he has a child?"

"When you say it like that, Regina, it sounds like I did it on purpose."

The house cleaner arched a brow. "Did you keep it a secret by accident?"

"Don't look at me like that," Flora said. Mateo grunted and reached for the spoonful of peaches still in Regina's paused hand. "Like I mentioned before, it's complicated. Hayes and I still have a lot of things to work out."

When the woman's eyes went from doubtful to hopeful, Flora held up a palm.

"Not like that. I mean we have a lot of logistics to work out as far as co-parenting goes. Like work schedules and shared responsibilities and, ultimately, what is best for Mateo."

No matter what the man said yesterday, Flora could still hear the conviction in Hayes's voice eighteen months ago when he'd told her didn't want kids. Right now, it was still a novelty for him. In a month, or in a year, who knew how he would feel? After he'd left last night, she'd looked up the name of his camp and was surprised to see that there were several of them across Texas. The man certainly had his hands full already and had no idea what it was like being a working parent. Especially a single working parent. What if he decided he couldn't handle it after all? That he wasn't meant to be a father?

"Right." Regina nodded as she handed the spoon to Mateo so he could practice feeding himself. "I can see how it would've been necessary to share a bottle of wine as you guys talked about visitation schedules. Totally logistical and not romantic at all."

So maybe there'd still been a little bit of physical chemistry between her and Hayes. There was still no way Flora was going to tell anyone about that passionate kiss last night. She didn't even want to think about it—or the way her body had pressed into his as his mouth reminded her of how skilled he was. Except she'd already thought of it at least twenty times this morning and she hadn't even had coffee yet.

"Your mama looks like she's got a lot on her mind today, Matty." Regina removed the bib and lifted him out of his high chair. "Why don't you hang out with me for a couple of hours while she calls your grandparents on her way to work. We can do some laundry, maybe go for a little walk and feed the ducks, and then I'll drop you off at the shop on my way to get more groceries? I have a feeling there's going to be a lot more cooking happening in this kitchen while your daddy is in town..."

Regina had said "in town." That told Flora the gossip mill had all but confirmed Hayes would only be here temporarily, so there was no reason for her to get worried about Mateo getting too attached to him.

"Last night was a onetime thing," she insisted. "I'm certainly not planning on cooking dinner for the man, let alone having him over for another meal."

Turned out, Flora may not have planned to cook for Hayes that night, but Regina certainly had.

In fact, there'd been no plan for him to come over for dinner at all. Yesterday, Hayes might've said, *I'll see you tomorrow* but Flora had been in a fog of passion and didn't even remember walking him to the door. He'd left in such a hurry after that kiss last night, they still hadn't exchanged phone numbers.

They did remedy that, though, when he stopped by

Lone Star Little Ones much later that morning. Flora could tell he was disappointed Mateo wasn't at the shop yet, which meant that he was more concerned about seeing their son rather than reliving last night's kiss. That was a good thing, she told herself. She offered to message him when Regina dropped off Mateo, but by the time that happened, he was in the middle of a prescheduled video meeting with his camp directors.

Hayes texted after his meeting and asked if he could bring dinner over again, and Flora really wanted to decline his offer because she didn't want to set a precedent. She didn't want anyone—including herself—to get too accustomed to these little visitations. Actually, that's how she forced herself to think about any future encounters with Hayes. They were simply *visitations* between him and Mateo. However, the baby's afternoon nap had been interrupted by Bettina, the high school junior who worked at Lone Star Little Ones in the afternoons. Or rather, by Bettina's boyfriend who had entered the store with half of the Emerald Ridge High School marching band for a very elaborate—and loud—promposal.

While Flora was happy for Bettina, who'd been talking about the prom for *months*, Mateo was less enthusiastic with the trombone solo and remained unusually fussy while she tried to finish the swimsuit inventory. So when Hayes's message about dinner came through, all Flora could think was that it would be really nice to have another set of hands tonight when it came to highchair feedings and bedtime routines.

It just so happened that Regina had also texted a photo of the tray of chicken enchiladas she'd prepped with detailed baking instructions. When Flora walked into the kitchen that evening with Mateo, she was glad she'd told Hayes not to bring any food.

"So much for not setting a precedent," she told her son, who was gnawing on the Stetson again. "Now your dad is going to think that we went out of our way to impress him with a home-cooked meal."

The doorbell rang before Flora could scold herself for how easily she'd just used the word *dad* in referring to a man who had only been present in her son's life for two days.

However, with the way Mateo lunged for Hayes the second she opened the door, coupled with the way he effortlessly hauled the squirming baby into his arms, it would soon get increasingly difficult to not think of the guy as her child's dad. Just like last night, the two seemed practically inseparable.

Thankfully, he'd worn a plain tee shirt this time with a faded pair of jeans, suggesting he hadn't gone out of his way to get dressed up. Although, he still looked just as good as he had last night.

"It smells amazing in here," Hayes said as Flora led him through the house toward the kitchen.

"I didn't cook." Her reply was immediate, her tone slightly sharp.

"I didn't say you did," Hayes spoke slowly, his tone confused.

"Regina might've gotten a little carried away and made enough food to feed an entire bunkhouse," Flora explained as they entered the kitchen. "That's what she used to do before coming to work for my family. She was a cook at a ranch where Manny used to train for… you know."

"She must've been close with him, too." Hayes had lowered his voice and looked around the room as though he was trying to determine if anyone else was there. "Is that why we're not allowed to say the word *rodeo*?"

She took a deep breath. "Sorry. I didn't mean to make it sound like I can't handle talking about my brother. It's been a long day and I'm trying to walk a delicate line between making you feel welcome to be a part of Mateo's life but not making you feel so welcome that you think I'm trying to bribe you into some family role that you're not ready for."

He lifted the foil cover from the baking dish still warm on the counter and inhaled. "I can always be bribed with homemade enchiladas."

Flora appreciated his attempt to diffuse her awkward comment with humor. But the conversation still needed to happen.

"What I'm trying to say is that I didn't plan all of this." She gestured at the stovetop with several cast-iron dishes containing rice, beans, elote, and whatever was in that blue-speckled pot on the back burner. Flora hadn't had time to uncover everything. "I'm happy to facilitate these visitations between you and Mateo, but I don't want you thinking I'm trying to lure you into anything more or have you worried that I'm under some impression we've just become one big happy family."

The corner of Hayes's mouth lifted in a slight smirk. "Does this little disclaimer have anything to do with the way you kissed me last night?"

"The way *I* kissed *you*?" Flora crossed her arms over her chest. She had to look up since Hayes, who was still holding Mateo, was standing so close to her. "I might've started things, but you were the one who took it to a whole other level."

"In that case, I'll keep it at *this* level in the future." Hayes dipped his head and softly pressed his lips against hers before quickly returning to his full six feet. "Now that we got all of the physical tension out of the way, can we eat?"

Mateo made a smacking sound of approval as he chewed on the brim of the hat, seemingly oblivious to the fact that his dad had just kissed his mom right there in the kitchen as if it was the most natural thing in the world.

"Hayes..." she started, then paused, trying to decide how big of a deal she wanted to make about boundaries when their nine-month-old was in the man's arms watching them. She saw the way his short sleeve had crept up over his tanned biceps and decided the boundaries were just as important for her as they were for him. "When I realized that I was going to be a single mom, I promised myself and our unborn child that I would never be one of those divorced parents who was always arguing with the ex about stuff in front of the kid."

"We're not divorced, Flora." Hayes easily shifted Mateo to his other arm, which displayed more flexing muscles. "And as far as I can tell, we're not arguing either."

"We're not arguing *yet*," she pointed out. "But if we don't lay out some ground rules soon, then things could get complicated."

"Oh, we're well past the complicated stage," he said as he walked toward the refrigerator. "Should I get the peas, or did you want me to feed Mateo something different tonight?"

She lifted her eyes toward the ceiling, inhaling through her nose and counting to five before releasing it. He was right. There was no way they were going to uncomplicate things with a simple talk about boundaries. Especially not before dinner.

Flora managed not to sigh when she finally said, "It's sweet potatoes tonight. With turkey."

"I hope he doesn't want to share. I like sweet potatoes a lot less than I like peas."

Hayes opened the refrigerator, and Flora was tempted to add another thing to the list of boundaries for successful co-parenting. *Don't make yourself at home in the other person's house.* Of course, that was slightly unfair given that she was insisting on having these visitations in her home since it was Mateo's normal environment. Hayes could easily argue that the goal was for him to be able to care for Mateo on his own without asking for help or permission for every little thing.

Besides, it was so nice to not have to walk him through the steps of how to heat baby food. In Flora's line of work, it was extremely common to hear mothers complain about carrying the mental load of the household and being the only parent who knew where the extra pacifiers were kept or when the diapers were running low.

So, with that in mind, she decided that rather than talk about boundaries, she should let Hayes figure out for himself that there was more to parenting than showing up when most of the work was already done.

She got down two plates from the cabinet and said, "I'm starving, and the enchiladas are getting cold. You think you can feed the baby while we eat our dinner at the same time?"

Hayes smile was a little too cocky. "No problem."

"You might think you want this tortilla chip, partner, but you nearly choked on that rice I gave you earlier. I'll be picking grains out of my hair all night."

Hayes thought it'd be a lot easier to use the "one bite for you, one bite for me" approach with Mateo like he had last night. However, he hadn't realized that would only work if he and the baby were eating the same food. Even when he'd been given his own spoon to hold, their son wasn't exactly happy that he couldn't try the corn or the shredded chicken on his dad's plate. Flora, on the other hand, had been able to enjoy her meal in peace as she discreetly shook her head every time Hayes was about to give their son a taste of something he didn't have enough teeth for.

Finally, he'd had to put his plate on the counter where it would be out of sight so that Mateo could focus on what was in front of him.

"Did you know he was going to do this?" Hayes asked Flora, who was moving around the kitchen, putting leftovers into containers.

"I had a feeling, which is why I normally eat when he's occupied with something else."

He returned to the high chair with a banana, which made Mateo kick out his bare feet in excitement. "So, you were making me be the bad guy who had to deprive him of your housekeeper's amazing cooking?"

"Not exactly." Flora smiled. "More like I was making you be the test subject. Eventually, I have to get him used to having meals with other people. Before, it'd been easier to meet up with friends or have business meetings at restaurants when I could time things around him napping in his car seat carrier. But his sleep schedule is changing and now that he's big enough to be sitting at the table—or at least in a high chair pushed up to the table—I wanted to see how he would do if I had to take him out somewhere."

Hayes hadn't ever given any thought to what parents had to go through when it came to altering their lifestyles to accommodate their children. Obviously, he'd been in restaurants where there'd been a crying baby or a toddler jumping up and down in the booth behind him. But it hadn't been *his* problem.

"So what you're saying is that we should take him out to a restaurant tomorrow night? As a trial run?"

She paused, a serving spoon halfway between the pan of enchiladas and a plastic container. "Together? In public? All three of us?"

"Why do you sound so terrified?" Hayes used the knife from his place setting to cut the banana into small chunks like Flora had done the previous evening. "I'll be there with you. We can tag team."

"But tomorrow is a Friday night."

"Yep. Friday usually comes after Thursday." He was waiting for her to make an excuse about why they shouldn't be seen in town together. When she resumed scooping leftovers, Hayes realized that her hesitation might not have anything to do with him. "Did you already have dinner plans for tomorrow?"

He didn't specifically ask about her dating life, but Flora was a beautiful, successful woman. If she hadn't had them yet, there'd soon be some offers. Hayes wouldn't think twice about asking a woman like her out, under different circumstances, obviously. Unfortunately, thinking about another man sharing the same experiences he wanted to share with the mother of his child made his jaw tighten.

"No, I don't have plans. But Fridays are pretty busy in Emerald Ridge with tourists and the weekenders coming to town. It might be a bit too chaotic to take a nine-month-old out to a restaurant where people are trying to enjoy their meals."

"Oh, come on. There are plenty of kid-friendly places we can take him. We'll go early, too, so we can beat the rush."

"'Beat the rush'?" Flora repeated, sealing two corn cobs in a plastic bag before adding it to the growing stack of leftovers. "You sound like Sue, who refuses to order anything that isn't on the early bird special menu."

"And you look like my mom's sister who refuses to let anyone leave her house without a bag of food containers that we have to promise to return."

"You *have* to take some of this back to the hotel with you. Otherwise, Regina will think you didn't get enough to eat."

Truthfully, Hayes only had time to eat about half the food on his plate and most of it had been cold when he'd finally managed a few bites. He'd left in a rush the night before and ended up calling room service for a burger because he was still hungry. He didn't want to make the same mistake tonight, which was part of the reason why he'd kissed Flora earlier in the evening. It was best to get all the awkwardness out of the way. The other part of the reason was that she'd looked so good in her form-fitting, sleeveless top and breezy, linen pants, he couldn't stop himself.

Mateo had made quick work of his bananas and was holding out his arms in what Hayes had learned was the sign for wanting to be picked up. He lifted his son out of his high chair.

And then the smell hit him.

"Oh, boy," Hayes exclaimed, trying not to plug his nose. "I've walked through dairy farms that smell like roses compared to this, partner."

Flora started toward them, then stopped and fanned her hand in front of her face. "Do you know where the wipes are?"

He didn't want to admit that this was his first dirty diaper, and he certainly didn't want to admit that he might need some help. "I saw them on the changing table in his nursery, but do you think there's going to be enough?"

Flora giggled, the sound immediately taking him back to that easygoing weekend he'd first met her. "If it takes more than three, you might as well use the handheld shower nozzle before filling the tub."

Hayes tried to remember how to get to Flora and Mateo's wing, but the house was pretty huge and his eyes were starting to water. He went down the wrong hallway and saw a large portrait on the wall. There were four kids, and he immediately recognized Flora as the one with braces and a lopsided ponytail. He didn't really know anything about two of her siblings, but he was pretty sure the taller teenager wearing the big silver belt buckle was her brother who'd passed away. Hayes had the exact same buckle, but he'd won his eight years later.

Feeling guilty for catching a glimpse of something so private, he immediately turned around and quickly found his way to the other side of the house. When it became apparent that the diaper hadn't been able to contain everything, Hayes went straight to the bathroom to get Mateo out of his soiled pants. It took incredibly strong gag reflexes and lots of warm water to get his son rinsed off enough to prevent the bubble bath from being counterproductive.

"Do you need any help?" Flora came into the bathroom after the worst was over. Yep, her carefree smile could still put him at ease.

"I put the dirty diaper in the trash can over there and double knotted the bag. I'm trying to soak the pants in the sink, but we may have to burn them."

"Well, he certainly smells better already. Good job, Dad."

Hayes could feel his chest expanding, even as he knew it was ridiculous to feel this much pride over handling something as minor as a diaper explosion. But it was the first time someone had called him *Dad* and it felt like he'd finally managed a task worthy of the title.

Again, there was a bottle waiting on the table beside the rocking chair after Hayes had bathed and dressed Mateo in his pajamas—only one snap left undone. Watching his son's sleepy eyes drift closed was one of the best feelings in the world. It was also a feeling that Hayes could get used to. Just like having dinner with Flora was becoming a little too comfortable.

When he met her in the sitting area outside the bedrooms, there wasn't any wine waiting for him this time. Or a carefree smile. Just a bag of what he assumed were leftovers sitting on the coffee table and his child's mother standing there with her arms tightly crossed in front of her chest.

Without Mateo acting as a buffer between them, Hayes suddenly didn't feel so at ease after all. Maybe he shouldn't have gone in for the casual kiss a couple of hours ago. Likely not wanting a repeat of last night's sofa activities, Flora intended to talk to him about boundaries and co-parenting before sending him on his way.

"Listen." He started before she could launch into a lecture. "I know that it's probably best if we try to keep all of the physical stuff between us out of the equation while we're navigating our new roles."

He saw her shoulders loosen, her arms falling to her sides, as though she could finally relax now that they were in agreement. It was almost as if she was relieved that she didn't have to admit that the chemistry they used to share was clearly still there. But not relieved enough to smile at him again like she had earlier.

Hayes lifted his chin defiantly. "I'm not saying that there won't be the occasional slip sometimes. Your body obviously has a mind of its own where I'm concerned and I'll try to be understanding if you accidentally grab my butt when we pass by each other in the kitchen. Or if I'm on the sofa and you fall into my lap and start making out with me again."

Flora slid her hands into her back pockets, causing her breasts to press against the ribbing of her thin, cotton tank. "Were you this cocky that weekend we first met?"

"No." He smiled. "I was way cockier. So were you, though."

She managed a half smirk before her expression grew

serious again. "That was back when I could afford to let my walls down a little. I can no longer do that since it's not just me I need to protect anymore. Mateo is my number one priority."

"He's my number-one priority, too, Flora. I want to protect him just as much as you do. How can I prove that I'm not going to shirk my responsibilities when it comes to our son?"

"Honestly? It's going to take more than a few nights of bedtime routines and diaper changes to convince me." Flora held up a palm when he opened his mouth to argue. "I'm not saying that you haven't taken this surprisingly well for a man who once claimed he never wanted children."

Hayes rolled his eyes. "I don't think those were my exact words, but it has been eighteen months, a concussion, and two major surgeries since then, so I can't remember what you might've heard."

Now Flora was the one to roll her eyes, but then she refocused her gaze and squared her toned, tan shoulders. "What I'm *trying* to say is that I can tell you want to be here for Mateo—physically. Right now, he's a baby and most of his needs require someone taking care of him. But what about when he's fifteen and he can peel his own bananas? He'll need advice on how to be a good teammate and friend. How to change a tire, shave and get over his first broken heart. Hayes… I need to know that you'll be here for him emotionally, too—so that Mateo knows he can always count on you."

Every muscle in his body became tense as he restrained himself from arguing that his son would always be able to rely on him. Emotionally and physically.

Instead, he threw his hands in the air, his palms slapping against his hips as he dropped them.

"If it takes eighteen years to prove myself to you and Mateo, then that's what it takes. Fatherhood was the furthest thing from my mind that weekend we met, so I likely said some things that made me sound like a selfish, arrogant cowboy. But I've been through a lot of shit since then, Flora. I've learned a lot about what I'm capable of and about the kind of man I *don't* want to be. Now I'm not accusing my father of being a complete deadbeat dad, especially because he supported us very well financially. But his secret lives meant he was gone far more often than he was present. I resented him for that back then." He drew in a deep ragged breath. "There's no way that I'm going to make the same mistakes and raise a child who resents me, too. It's the same reason why I'm so insistent on making sure everyone knows that Mateo is mine. I'm done with secrets."

"I can appreciate you feeling that way," Flora replied, her mouth softer, but still serious. "But you're not the only person in this equation. We all have feelings about what we think is best."

"Like how you thought not telling me about my child was best?"

"Like how I thought you wouldn't care one way or the other," she shot back. "But I was *wrong*, Hayes. Sometimes, we're going to get it wrong. There's no perfect way to raise a child. All we can do is keep showing up."

"Then I'll keep showing up." Hayes walked toward the table to pick up the bag of leftovers. "Including tomorrow at five for our early bird dinner at an actual restaurant. I'll drive."

# Chapter Six

Flora had packed Mateo's diaper bag with several spare sets of clothes, his favorite stuffed animal, a box of teething biscuits and several small toys to keep him entertained. When Hayes arrived promptly at five the following evening to pick them up, she found out that she wasn't the only who'd come prepared.

"I bought a new car seat today. Shelby said it's the same one she registered for, and her fiancé, Cameron, showed me how to install it."

"So all of your family knows about Mateo?" Flora asked, staring at the way the back of his jeans molded around his sculpted—

Whoops. She missed the bottom porch step and nearly face-planted onto the brick path before catching herself. Thankfully, he hadn't seen and she was able to quickly resume following him to his truck.

"I've told the ones that I want to know," he said somewhat cryptically.

Flora waited until they were inside the vehicle, Mateo's car seat straps tripled-checked for tightness, before telling Hayes about the unexpected customers who came by today. "Jillian Fortune stopped by my shop this afternoon. She was with another woman who might've been your half sister. Madeline, I think?"

"I'm sorry about that." He slowly pulled out of the driveway. "I should've given you the heads-up."

"No need to apologize." Flora glanced at the speedometer and saw that Hayes was driving at least ten miles per hour under the speed limit. At this rate, they weren't going to make it to the restaurant in time for the early bird specials. "I'm only bringing it up so that you'll be understanding when you check your social media page and see that both Sue and Regina are now following you."

"Good to know, although, you should probably tell them that I'm rarely active on social media. My dad was really strict about Penn and me not having any access to online networks when we were teens. Other than telling people we weren't related to 'those' Fortunes, we really weren't allowed to talk about ourselves or our family. Now I know why. Anyway, old habits die hard and I hardly ever look at my page. My agent used to handle it for me, but now there's a public relations person at Saddle Up who runs it."

In Flora's line of work, branding was such an important part of promoting her store, she knew more about social media collaborations than she wanted to admit. That's why she didn't want to tell Hayes that Bettina, her teenage employee, had suggested some sort of collaboration between Lone Star Little Ones and a former rodeo star.

"So did Jillian or Madeline say anything to you?" Hayes asked, bring her back to the present conversation.

"Not really. Sue was helping them pick out gifts for Shelby's baby shower. At first, they kept looking over at Mateo and I could tell they wanted to ask about him." Flora gave him a sideways glance, trying to gauge his reaction. "But within a few minutes, an older woman joined them and they both tried to avoid looking in my or Mateo's direction at all. The woman introduced herself as Taffy Fortune and then told Sue she was Archibald's third wife."

"Taffy definitely likes to make her presence known," Hayes murmured as he let every other car at the four-way stop proceed before them. "She probably showed up so she could guilt Madeline into getting her an invitation to Shelby's baby shower."

"I'm not sure the guilt trip worked since she didn't buy a gift or anything else. The only reason I'm bringing it up is because I got the impression that your sisters didn't want Taffy to know that Mateo might be related to you."

"Hmm," was all he said in response. Although, he seemed to carefully consider her words as he slowly made a right turn.

After the fifth car passed them, Flora finally asked, "Have you always been this…uh…cautious of a driver?"

"I'm not taking any chances with my son in the car."

"Hayes, I appreciate you wanting to be careful, but I drive this same route with him every day and it shouldn't take—" she glanced at the clock on the dash "—twenty minutes to get to Francesca's Bar and Grill."

He kept his strong, sun-bronzed hands in the ten and two positions on the steering wheel but increased the speed slightly while remaining in the slow lane. "So how did your parents take the news that Mateo's dad was back in the picture?"

"Pretty much exactly how I expected they would,"

she replied, not wanting to admit that all she'd told them was that she'd run into Mateo's father. She didn't divulge Hayes's name and she definitely didn't admit that they'd spent the last two evenings together. "I told them that I wasn't sure how long you'd be in town and that there was no need for them to rush home from their trip. But I should probably warn you that both my sister and my brother have already booked flights to come to Emerald Ridge for Mateo's first birthday party."

Now he had fair warning in case he wanted to high-tail it out of town before her family arrived.

"Did you already start making arrangements for his party?" Hayes asked. "Is there a theme? I was thinking we could ask Madeline to plan it at one of my ranches—"

"It's still three months away," Flora interrupted before party planning talks got out of control. He was supposed to be nervous about meeting family, not offering to host them for a party. "A lot of things can change in three months."

"Nobody knows that better than me," Hayes said with a sigh as he pulled into a parking spot in front of the family-style restaurant. "Okay, who is ready for our first family outing at a sit-down restaurant?"

*Not me*, Flora thought to herself as she watched a dad hold open the door for three kids wearing matching soccer jerseys. But Mateo responded with some nonsensical baby babbling, which only seemed to motivate Hayes into thinking this was going to be a fun experience.

"Let's go, partner," he said, lifting the baby out of his seat while balancing the overstuffed diaper bag strap on his shoulder.

Flora, her hands completely free, had already forgotten how simple life could be when all she had to carry was a small purse. Hayes held open the front door for her and Mateo had impeccable timing when he took the black Stetson from his father's head the second they entered the restaurant.

In his boots and button-up shirt, Hayes looked like he could've been a professional model for a cowboy ad. His slightly tousled hair only made him seem more human. *More attractive.* Flora watched as several heads turned in their direction and knew it was too late to run now. Forcing a smile on her face, she asked the hostess for a table with a high chair.

They'd made it halfway through the dining area before being recognized.

Martina Leonetti, who'd recently stepped down at Leonetti Vineyards so that her four children could take over the business, waved politely. Her eighty-something year old father Enzo, though, called out to Flora who stopped long enough to exchange greetings as Hayes continued to the table and got Mateo into a seat. Mateo didn't seem to know what to look at first. There was so much going on inside the restaurant, especially with the three soccer kids who had been seated at the table across from them and were very animated—and loud—with their recap of the game they'd just won.

The teenage waitress had just finished taking their drink order when several kids from the high school marching band came into the building blaring their instruments as they assisted with another promposal.

Mateo, who thankfully hadn't been napping this time, moved his body back and forth, trying to dance along to a drum-heavy rendition of a Taylor Swift song. When the band finished with a final crash of the cymbals, Hayes asked Flora, "Is this an Emerald Ridge thing?"

"I think it's the new rage with high schoolers everywhere." Flora explained how the girl who worked in her store had been on the receiving end of a similar display. "Apparently, the band members have been hired by several boys in town who want an elaborate way to ask girls to the prom."

"Back in my day," Enzo Leonetti said loud enough for everyone seated around the octogenarian to hear, "if a fella wanted to ask a gal out on a date, he just asked her. Maybe show up at her house with a nice bottle of Chianti if he wanted to score points with her parents. Now everyone has to make a big scene and record it on a video, broadcasting it to the dang World Wide Web."

"Since high schoolers can't buy wine yet, Dad, they have to find more modern ways to impress their dates," Martina said. "I hope all the camera phones pointed in this direction didn't record you scowling the whole time."

Enzo made a dismissive gesture with his age-spotted hand, then turned toward Flora and Hayes and said, "Son, that baby is chewing on your hat."

"Yes, sir, he is," Hayes replied. "He's teething. But don't worry, I double-checked on the World Wide Web to make sure none of the material in my hat would be any worse for him than a stuffed animal."

Flora's heart swelled at the knowledge that Hayes was going out of his way to make sure their child was safe and happy. And that he'd politely redirected any potential criticism of their parenting choices.

The older man continued to stare in their direction,

though. A moment later, he pointed a finger at Hayes. "You look familiar."

He smiled politely. "Maybe you saw me in a rodeo competition."

"Nope, that's not it." Enzo squinted through his bifocals. "You look like that Fortune fella. The one with the local ranch named after his daughters."

*Fortune and Daughters Ranch.* Flora had been in Emerald Ridge long enough to hear of the ranch well before Shelby and Jillian Fortune had been to her shop. Until now, she hadn't realized that the name of the ranch could be perceived as a slight to Archibald's other children.

Hayes scratched his chin, then replied, "Nobody's ever told me that."

Flora had done a Google search of Hayes's father today after Jillian and Madeline had stopped by the store. In all of the photos she'd seen of Archibald Fortune, there wasn't a single one that resembled Hayes.

Any further observations by Enzo Leonetti were thankfully interrupted when their waitress, who was still smiling after her public prom invitation, returned with their drinks and took their order. Mateo had given up the cowboy hat for a teething biscuit that he sucked on while being mesmerized by the television screen over the bar area.

"I'm guessing he doesn't watch a lot of TV yet," Hayes remarked before taking a drink of his sweet tea. "That's pretty unusual in this digital age."

"I know. There are so many opinions out there about screen time and, as much as I want to follow all the pediatric recommendations, who's to say that in a few months I won't be planting him in front of a cartoon so that I can take a shower in peace. Especially if he's easily entertained by…" Flora angled her head so she could see whatever had her son so entranced and then groaned when she saw cowboys on horses chasing after a calf. "I thought it was on a sports channel."

"Rodeo *is* a sport."

"It can also become a lifestyle. One that I don't want my son to pursue."

"You know what I find funny," Hayes said, showing zero humor on his face. "How you can be so dead set against everything related to riding and roping and yet your store logo is a little cowboy with a lasso."

"I'm born and raised in Texas, Hayes. Obviously, I'm not against roping and riding—or even cowboys. You mentioned before that your camps also teach kids about the ranching industry, which I totally respect and support. But I do think playing cowboy at rodeo events is an unnecessary risk." She took a sip of her unsweetened tea but continued before he could respond. "And before you give me a lecture about rodeos being a way for cowboys to enjoy some recreation outside of work, I know the history and I even understand some of the appeal. My brother loved being on a ranch, he loved the roping and riding, and he loved the animals." Emotion clogged her throat but she forced herself to carry on in a quiet voice that wouldn't draw any attention their way. "There's no doubt in my mind that he could've been extremely successful as a rancher if that had been his chosen profession. But I can still wish that he would've taken up yoga or swimming or any other hobby that didn't involve a fifteen-hundred-pound angry bull charging at him."

Instead of arguing with her, though, Hayes reached

across the table and used his thumb to stroke her hand, which was still gripping her iced tea. Flora exhaled and slowly relaxed her fingers.

A commercial must've come on the TV because Mateo dropped his slobbery biscuit and looked around the restaurant for a new source of entertainment.

"Did you pack some jars of food for him?" Hayes needed both hands to look through the diaper bag, which was closest to his seat since he'd carried it inside.

Flora offered to feed Mateo, but Hayes was very insistent on taking charge. He might've only been doing it to prove that he could handle his son's needs whether they were at her house or out in public. Or maybe he knew that he'd been the one who'd pushed to dine out at a restaurant and he didn't want her to regret being talked into it. Either way, she wasn't going to complain because it meant that she was able to eat her dinner while it was still warm.

Mateo's first time eating at a restaurant actually ended up being much more successful than she'd anticipated. Probably because Hayes was proving himself to be very cool under pressure. By the time the check arrived, Flora was thinking that maybe this had been a good idea after all. She took Mateo to the restroom to try to wash most of the mashed potatoes off his hands and face, and when she returned to the table, it became clear that whatever lighthearted family moment they'd been experiencing with Hayes was now over.

He was still outwardly calm, because of course he was. But he was staring at a message on his phone, eyes narrowed and jaw clenched. The second he looked up and saw her, he shoved the phone into his shirt pocket.

"What's wrong?" Flora asked as she passed Mateo to him so that she could pack up the diaper bag.

"Nothing," he answered quietly. Obviously, he hadn't meant what he'd said yesterday about no more secrets because there was clearly something that had happened, yet he didn't want her to know about.

When they got in the truck, she tried again. "Are you sure you're not too upset to drive?"

Hayes frowned. "Why would I be upset?"

"I'm not sure. You got super quiet after looking at your phone inside the restaurant. And because you're literally scowling right now."

"My sister Jillian sent a text in our family group chat. It kind of caught me by surprise. But I'm good. Who wants to stop for ice cream on the way home?"

Hayes hadn't been joking when he'd told Flora that he didn't have social media as a teen because he'd always been cautioned about not speaking publicly about his family. In fact, it had been so ingrained in him, it felt unnatural to go into too much detail about Jillian's text when Flora asked what was wrong. Especially at the restaurant with curious diners possibly listening in. And then in the truck on the way back to her house, he thought that bringing up his father's past would only dampen the mood. They'd been doing so well at dinner, just him and Flora and Mateo. She'd even let him take her hand across the table when she'd been talking about her brother.

Hayes didn't want to spoil the good vibe. Or worse. Make her think that he was bringing too much drama and baggage into her life.

He helped with the nighttime routine again, but as soon as his son had fallen asleep in his arms, Hayes laid him in his crib and then told Flora he would reach out the following day. She nodded and he was relieved she didn't ask him again if everything was okay. So relieved that the soft goodbye kiss he'd given her lasted a few seconds longer than he'd intended. He'd pulled himself back before he changed his mind and carried her straight to her bedroom. Being in her home, in the comfortable environment she'd created for her and Mateo, he didn't think he could've downplayed everything running through his head right now.

He waited until he was out of sight from the Rodriguez home before pulling over along the side of the quiet neighborhood street so that he could reread the text from Jillian and then the subsequent messages from Shelby and Madeline. Penn hadn't replied yet. So that was who Hayes decided to call first on his drive back to the hotel.

"Took you long enough," his brother said by way of greeting when he answered.

"I was out to dinner with Flora and Mateo."

"Right." Penn replied and Hayes could picture the way his brother was likely pacing back and forth in some hotel room in whatever city he was in. "I got the picture you sent me yesterday. Cute kid. Hopefully, he inherited his favorite uncle's brains."

"You'll need to come meet him in person before you can award yourself the favorite uncle title. Flora's brother Sebastian might've already claimed that role."

"At this rate, there's no telling how many potential uncles Mateo might have. But at least we confirmed that Dad didn't have any siblings of his own."

*"We?"* Hayes scanned the intersection before proceeding through the green light. "I'm pretty sure our half sister Jillian was the one who discovered it. You haven't exactly been willing to help, remember?"

"Just because I'm not physically holed up in Emerald Ridge with you doesn't mean I'm not paying attention. Plus, I don't think Dad kept it a secret that he was an orphan."

"Yeah, but I always assumed he'd never known his parents at all. According to Jillian's text, though, Dad was fourteen when they died. Why didn't he ever mention them?"

Penn's laugh on the other end of the line sounded forced and lacked any humor. "Apparently, there were a lot of things Dad never mentioned."

Jillian's message had also explained that Clyde and Cass Fortune, a couple whose small parcel of land near the tracks had been foreclosed upon over sixty years ago, were actually their grandparents. Clyde and Cass were completely broke when they died. There were no other relatives, and no clues about what had happened to Archibald between age fourteen and his mid-twenties when he started his company.

A horn honked behind Hayes, startling him out of his deep thought, and he moved over to the slow lane. Mateo was no longer in his car seat, but the outline of the empty headrest served as a reminder that he needed to stay focused.

"Everything okay over there?" Penn asked.

"Yeah. I'm just in autopilot mode, trying to process everything."

"You've got to stop overthinking all of this, man." His

brother made it sound like there was an on/off switch that could be flipped on a whim. "The more you guys keep digging, the more dirt you're going to unearth."

"Yeah, Penn. That's how digging works. And if it were only about me, I'd gladly walk away from this hole that's only getting deeper and deeper. We both know I don't need Dad's money to cover my personal expenses. I could easily land a job as a commentator or a judge or even a stock contractor that allows me to make a good living in the rodeo circuit. But running a nonprofit organization takes money and horse camps aren't cheap." He tightened his grip on the steering wheel and blew out a rough breath. "I'll eventually need the inheritance if I want to keep Saddle Up going for more than a few years. Plus, this isn't just about us kids. Mom was raising us on her own while Dad was out making a mockery of their wedding vows. She deserves her share."

Penn was so quiet, Hayes thought his phone reception had cut out. Finally, his brother said, "I've got to head into a design meeting with the architects for my next hotel. Send me another pic of my nephew when you get a chance."

The call disconnected and Hayes didn't feel any less frustrated than he had since getting their half sister's message earlier. He knew Penn was just as affected as the rest of them were, but he didn't want to push his own feelings and his experiences on his brother.

The truth was that Hayes was once again stunned by the latest revelation. While Archibald may not have spent much time at their home with them, he had still felt the man's presence throughout his childhood. From the big family portrait hanging over the mantel in their living room, to his dad's private study filled with books on jet propulsion and framed prints of Fortune Air's flight routes, to the luxury sports car parked next to his mom's SUV in the oversize garage—only driven when his dad was working at his Houston office—Archibald was there, even when he wasn't.

The man who hadn't attended a single rodeo event Hayes had ever competed in, was the same man who'd bought his other family a stable full of Arabian horses housed at a ranch he'd named Fortune and Daughters. The father who used to lecture his sons about the importance of a valuable education, never left a single hint of where he'd gone to high school. Or if he'd gone at all. Was the framed college degree on the wall in his dad's study back home a fake? Did he have duplicate copies hanging in the other two houses where he'd lived with his other families?

Hayes pulled into the parking lot at the Emerald Ridge Hotel, completely shaken by how little he knew the man who was his father.

The following morning, Hayes decided that he was getting pretty tired of hotel coffee and the same breakfast menu. Jumping in the shower, he found himself wondering what the morning routine was like at Flora's house. There was a very expensive- and high-tech-looking espresso machine in the Rodriguezes' state-of-the-art kitchen. Was Flora making herself something with lots of caffeine and steamed milk? Could Mateo eat scrambled eggs yet?

Hayes had only shared evening meals with them and suddenly he wanted to know what the rest of their day consisted of. Being the type of guy who got a thrill by jumping into a narrow chute with some of the meanest horses in the world, it was only natural for him to throw himself into this unknown arena of fatherhood. However, Flora was determined to ease them both into the co-parenting thing, and he didn't think he'd earned the right to override her wishes.

Of course, Flora knew just as well he did that when it came to each other, neither one of them had ever been good at easing into situations. The night they first met was proof of that.

Plus, Hayes's mom *had* sent another message this morning asking if she could meet her grandson when she came into town again. And he'd pretty much used his son as an incentive to get Penn to finally come to Emerald Ridge. Obviously, his mom and brother would be eager to meet his baby. Hopefully, Flora would understand that the Fortunes weren't trying to overwhelm either her or, more importantly, Mateo. They were just trying to make up for lost time.

After getting dressed, Hayes decided to skip breakfast at the hotel and walked over to the Coffee Connection instead. He was a few feet away from the entrance when his half sister Madeline came out the doors, a coffee in one hand and her phone in the other. She was using her thumb to type and wasn't paying attention when she nearly plowed into Hayes.

"Heads up," he said, jumping to the side with the same quick reflexes he'd honed on the rodeo circuit.

"Sorry about that," Madeline said when she recovered from nearly spilling her coffee all over him. "I was looking up an address and trying to figure out how long it would take me drive to the outskirts of town. But I'm not sure I can make it before I need to meet with the caterers I'm interviewing for Kate Fortune's party."

He knew Madeline had once owned a successful party-planning business in Dallas. However, she was new to Emerald Ridge and hadn't built up her client list yet. It made Hayes wonder why someone like Kate Fortune—who wasn't a direct relation to them as far as anyone could tell—would insist on Madeline planning an event as monumental as her one-hundredth birthday celebration. Not that Madeline couldn't do it. But there were too many weird coincidences happening lately to overlook any possible connection to his father's past.

"Why are you going so far out of town?" Hayes had a habit of looking up potential properties for his next camp locations and was already working with his real estate agent to find something near Emerald Ridge that might be suitable. "There's not much out there besides a bunch of cows on some remote ranches. Most of the property owners in places like that don't want people dropping in out of the blue. Do you have a lead about something?"

"Not about anything related to Dad," Madeline said quickly, and Hayes had to remind himself that she was talking about his dad as well as hers. He was still getting used to the thought that people other than he and Penn had called Archibald that. "Kate thinks her great-great-grandniece might live out there. Fun fact, Kate Fortune is apparently related to Susannah Simmons, the famous actress."

Hayes had so much going on with his own life right now, it was hard to keep track of what was happening in everyone else's worlds, as well. But he wanted to be a good brother, especially to Madeline, who was a year younger and had been raised as an only child by a mother who wasn't the easiest to deal with.

"Is this the great-great-grandniece who seems to want nothing to do with Kate?"

"Yes," Madeline said. "Or at least maybe. I'm not convinced Susannah's gotten my messages, though. I'm thinking about driving out there and just not leaving until the woman answers the door."

"She's a famous celebrity who probably values her privacy. Don't you think that's a little too…uh…stalkerish?"

Madeline grimaced. "I didn't mean that the way it sounded. I just think that if I go in person, I can better explain to Susannah how much it would mean to her aunt if she attended the party."

"Or you could find out that she has a perfectly good reason for being estranged from this supposed aunt of hers." Hayes stopped himself before repeating Penn's line last night about digging too much and uncovering more dirt.

"That's true. But Kate is my first client in Emerald Ridge, and back in Dallas, my business has a reputation for delivering for our clients. So even if I can't make it happen, I at least need to be able to say I did everything in my power to ensure this event surpasses Kate's expectations."

"Fine," Hayes said, trying to be understanding but unable to shake off the protective older brother role he'd never experienced since he was used to being the younger brother. "But I'm going with you. Just in case there's someone out at the ranch who plans to use any means necessary to keep trespassers off their property."

"You're probably right," Madeline admitted, then glanced at the clock on her screen. "But I don't think I'll have enough time to go today. What's next week looking like for you?"

"I'm meeting with the private investigator again on Monday and I might have to fly to Montana on Thursday to look at a possible site for the next Saddle Up location." It took a few minutes for them to figure out a day that would work best for both of their schedules and they locked it in before Madeline rushed off to her next appointment.

Hayes walked into Coffee Connection thinking that his new sisters were so much more agreeable than Penn. Definitely easier to get along with. Before placing his order, he decided to send Flora a text to see what she and Mateo had planned for today. And if she wanted him to bring anything for breakfast.

## *Chapter Seven*

"My mom will be in town next week and asked if she could meet Mateo," Hayes told Flora as they sat outside at a patio table in her backyard. Really, *backyard* was an understatement considering the wide expanse of grass gave way to one of the most beautiful views in Emerald Ridge beyond their open property line.

It was Flora's favorite spot to spend the morning on her days off. However, now that she had a nine-month-old, breakfast on the patio had become too much of a chore. Especially when she had to haul everything out here from the kitchen.

When Hayes offered to bring over something from the coffee shop, though, Flora'd decided that it might be worth the trouble to set up an impromptu outdoor dining experience. Now that they'd finished eating, the mention of his mom coming into town so soon sent off warning bells in her mind. Had she just been easily bamboozled by the offer of a double chocolate chip muffin?

Flora lifted a restless Mateo out of his high chair and set him on the blanket she'd spread on the grass earlier, then asked, "How would that work?"

"I'm guessing that I'd say something along the lines of 'Mom, this is your grandson Mateo.'" Hayes had followed them and sat down next to the baby. "A formal handshake is probably out of the question, although he's getting much better at giving high fives."

As if to prove it, he held up a palm in front of Mateo and was rewarded with a sticky fist bump of sorts. Flora went back to the table to get some wipes from the diaper bag she'd brought outside with them.

"I know how introductions work," she said, passing Hayes a wipe so he could clean the applesauce residue off his and Mateo's hands. "I meant, would she come here to my house or do you think it would be better for us to go to a neutral location like the park or something?"

"Us?" Hayes lifted one brow, his teasing smirk making her tummy do somersaults. "Are you saying that you're ready to meet my mom, too?"

"Not the way you're implying. I guess I figured that I'd likely need to be there too since you haven't babysat Mateo on your own yet."

"Fathers don't babysit their own children, Flora."

She cringed at her poor choice of words. "I know. I can't believe I even said it that way. I hope you know that it has nothing to do with me not trusting you with him. You're actually way better with him than I'd thought you'd be."

"I'm going to take that as a compliment, even though there was a slight backhandedness to it."

"You probably think I'm being controlling, but I'm a first-time mother, Hayes. And I've been doing it on my own for the most part. So please be patient with me while I learn to share some of the responsibility."

"I get it. We're both new to this and I don't want you thinking I'm over here making jokes when I should be taking things seriously." Rubbing the back of his neck with one hand, he admitted gruffly, "Sometimes it feels like you and I know each other so well. And then there's other times when it feels like we're complete strangers."

"I can certainly relate to that," she agreed. But she didn't add that last night had definitely felt like one of those times they were strangers. Hayes had gone quiet the moment he'd received that message from his sister and he still hadn't told her what it was about. Not that it was any of her business—or that she wanted it to be.

"Easy, partner." Hayes kept Mateo from toppling over face-first when the baby leaned forward to reach one of the toys in front of him. "We don't want you getting any bruises on your noggin before you meet Gigi."

"Gigi?" Flora asked.

"I know." Hayes rolled his eyes. "Apparently, that's what my mom picked out for her 'grandma' name. Why? Did your mom already call dibs on Gigi?"

"No. My mom thinks she's going to be Glamma, but I warned her that babies take a while to get that L sound and she might end up as a Gamma. My brother Sebastian already changed her name in the family group chat to the Greek symbol."

"I'm glad my mom isn't the only one who's put so much thought into it." He laughed. "She suggested I start practicing Gigi with Mateo now. Her dad, who was extremely formal, wanted us to call him Grandfather Morgan. But it was too much of a mouthful for me and Penn, so we just called him Twinkie."

Flora laughed. "Why Twinkie?"

"He always had a box of snack cakes he kept hidden in the pantry because my grandmother didn't like him eating processed food. I guess I inherited that trait from him."

"Are your grandparents still around?" she asked.

"No. They passed away when I was eight."

"What about your dad's parents?"

"I didn't know them." Hayes's expression became unreadable and he quickly changed the subject. "Anyway, so about my mom coming into town next week… I'd like for her to meet *both* you and Mateo. If that's okay with you."

Flora had obviously been in relationships where she'd met the guy's parents, but Hayes wasn't her boyfriend. It shouldn't be any different than when she'd met Sue's ninety-year-old mother at the store. So then why did the thought of meeting his mom suddenly make Flora's nerve endings crackle? Probably because she wanted to make a good impression. She wasn't just selling clothes and baby gear—she was selling herself as a *good mother* who was raising this woman's grandchild.

Forcing a smile, she nodded. "Of course I'm okay with that. Would Wednesday evening work?"

"I'll check," Hayes said, then pulled out his phone. After sending a text message, he snapped a photo of Mateo, who had maneuvered himself onto his belly and was rocking back and forth trying to reach a stuffed giraffe.

"He's getting really close to crawling soon," Flora explained. She helped position the baby's knees and hands so he could get more leverage. She heard the sound of Hayes's camera shutter and looked up to see that he was holding the phone angle at a distance. "Did you just take a picture of me?"

"Technically, I was taking a picture of my son and you happened to be in the shot."

*"Happened to be?"* She arched her eyebrows. "I'm pretty sure you aimed the lens in my direction on purpose."

"You're making it sound like I'm some sort of weirdo trying to sneak a photo of you." Hayes stood up and took several steps back. "If I really wanted a picture of you, Flora, I'd stand back here and say one, two, three."

The shutter went off again and he had the audacity to chuckle.

"Hayes!" she groaned. "You could've at least given me more warning. My mouth was probably hanging wide-open."

"Your mouth is perfect."

His words set off a fluttering sensation in her lower extremities and she knew better than to tell him he was standing too far away for her to see the screen. The last thing she needed was for him to bring the temptation closer.

Especially since he wasn't looking at the photo on the screen either. He was staring right at her lips. "But I'll take another one with more warning this time."

Flora almost picked up Mateo to hold his tiny body in front of her to ensure that their son was the main focus of the picture, as well as Hayes's reason for being here. But he'd finally scooted himself a few inches forward to close the distance between him and the desired toy. Instead, she folded her hands in her lap and gave what she thought was a demure smile. She heard the click at the exact second Mateo reached the giraffe.

"Now *that* was a great shot," Hayes said as he returned

to the blanket. He even handed his phone to Flora so she could give her approval.

"It really is," she said as she used two fingers on his screen to zoom in closer. Mateo was definitely the focal point and she was merely in the background. She wasn't sure if she was relieved or disappointed. Definitely relieved, she reminded herself. "Did you take a photography class or something?"

"More like I grew up attending the Damaris Fortune Art Institute. My mom was always trying to expose us to different mediums. I'm horrible with watercolors and sculptures, but I somehow managed to learn my way around a camera."

Flora still had his phone in her hands when she stood up and said, "Your turn. Say 'cheese.'"

But instead of smiling, Hayes quickly scooped up Mateo, who had just belly-crawled his way to the edge of the blanket and was about to shove a handful of grass into his mouth.

"Nice save, Dad," Flora said. She'd accidentally called him that a couple of days ago and had to warn herself to take things slower. However, it had always been impossible to take things slow when she was with him. Besides, the more time Hayes spent with Mateo, the more he seemed like…a dad. "Let's try for less of an action shot this time."

Hayes was holding Mateo in his lap and both of them looked up at the camera with their matching blue eyes. Flora wasn't really paying attention to the way she'd angled the camera or how many times she tapped the shutter. She couldn't stop thinking about how perfect they looked together—father and son.

Flora had a slight catch in her throat as she returned to the blanket and said, "Here, make sure there's one of these that you like. If not, I can take more..."

Hayes's fingers touched hers as he took the phone from her hand, sending a jolt of awareness through her body. She dared a peek at his expression to see if he was experiencing the same physical intensity she was.

Instead of passion, though, his eyes were squeezed shut and he started laughing so hard, Mateo had twisted around to stare at him.

"What's so funny?" Flora asked.

He turned the phone around. "Whose dog is this in the background?"

Mr. Paul's bichon frise had sneaked through the short hedge that separated their yards and was squatting as he made a deposit on the Rodriguezes' lawn.

"That's Velvet, our neighbor's dog. For some reason, he seems to prefer our grass to his own." The dog in question had finished his business and ran over to their blanket, much to Mateo's delight. "He's normally not this friendly."

"Really?" Hayes let Velvet sniff his hand and the dog immediately rolled onto his back. "He seems pretty friendly to me."

Flora watched in amazement as he rubbed the pooch's belly, then took Mateo's hand in his own and showed him how to gently pet his white, curly fur. It was a moment too adorable not to capture, so she took Hayes's phone, which was still on the camera setting, and gently eased away so she could snap another photo.

She'd taken several shots when Mr. Paul crossed into the backyard calling for his dog.

"Velvet's over here," Flora told her older neighbor, who walked right past the fresh pile of poop without giving it a second glance.

It was quickly apparent that Mr. Paul was less concerned with retrieving his wayward dog and more interested in getting a good look at Flora's visitor. "And who do we have here?"

Hayes stood, taking Mateo with him. He extended a hand and said, "Good Morning, sir. I'm Hayes Fortune."

Flora finished the introductions by saying, "Hayes, this is our neighbor, Mr. Paul. He's on the advisory council for our neighborhood homeowners association."

The man shook hands with Hayes.

"And I see you've already met my little prince, Velvet." The dog had wandered over to the patio table and was licking something on the ground under Mateo's high chair. "He likes to greet all the newcomers to our little corner of Emerald Ridge."

Flora tried not to roll her eyes. If by "greet" Mr. Paul meant *excessively bark at*, then yes, Velvet was the biggest greeter of all.

"Fortune, huh?" Mr. Paul continued as he openly studied Hayes and Mateo. "You one of those new ones related to Agatha's girls?"

As much as Flora wanted to apologize for her neighbor's blatant nosiness, she also took a step closer, wanting to hear how Hayes explained about the situation. He really hadn't said much about his family since that first night he was in town.

"I am," was the only response Hayes gave.

Flora immediately felt a wave of guilt for succumbing to the curiosity like all the other gossips in town.

"And judging by the color of your eyes," Mr. Paul squinted, "I'm guessing you're related to this little fella, as well."

"I can see why you're on the homeowner's association." Hayes smiled politely. "Nothing gets by you, sir."

"I guess you'll be moving in pretty soon, then." Mr. Paul had leaped to that conclusion awfully quickly. Before Flora could correct her neighbor, though, he was walking toward the patio. "Velvet, stop eating that."

The dog had jumped onto a chair and had its two front paws on Mateo's high chair, finishing off whatever food remained on the tray. Hayes, with Mateo pointing and babbling, went to help the older man retrieve his dog.

Flora felt something vibrate in her hand and looked at the phone screen. The notification came with a preview message and she read the words.

Sorry you guys, but my mom is on her high horse about something and is insisting we meet at the hotel tomorrow for some sort of emergency family meeting.

Why would the Rodriguezes need to have a family meeting at a hotel?

It wasn't until she saw the name of the sender—Madeline Fortune—that Flora realized she was still holding Hayes's phone from when she'd taken photos earlier. Heat raced up her cheeks as she flushed with embarrassment at reading a message intended for someone else.

Luckily, Hayes was distracted by Mateo, who was kicking his feet and gurgling out some encouraging gibberish to Velvet as the dog ran away from its owner with half of an almond croissant hanging out of its mouth.

"I hope you didn't want the rest of your breakfast," Hayes muttered to Flora when the dog went under the hedge with Mr. Paul following behind at a much slower pace. "Velvet moved from the high chair to the top of the table with lightning speed and precision."

"No, I was done." She swallowed down a bubble of shame as she passed Hayes his phone. "You have a message. I accidentally read it thinking I was holding my own phone."

Flora wasn't sure if the frown on Hayes's face was because she'd looked at his phone or because of the actual message itself. He tapped something and then slid the phone into his back pocket.

"If you need privacy to respond, Mateo and I can clean up here."

"Nah, I'm good," he said, but Flora's gut was telling her that something was wrong.

"Are you sure?" She knew she was pushing, but if something big was happening in his life, it could affect Mateo. Or at least his visitation with Mateo. "Your sister said it was an emergency."

"No, my sister said *her mom* thinks something is an emergency. Taffy can be pretty dramatic, though, and likes to cause a scene. I'm not too concerned."

Mateo yawned and put his head on Hayes's shoulder.

"You ready for a nap, partner?" he asked the baby who answered with several long blinks. "Should I put him down in his crib?"

"That would be awesome," Flora said. "I'll clean up here."

She expected Hayes to come into the kitchen once Mateo was down for his nap. After thirty minutes, though, she went to the nursery to check on them and saw Hayes in the oversize chair, his son cradled in his arms. Both of them sound asleep.

First a leisurely breakfast on the back patio, followed by a midday nap? Flora couldn't remember the last time she'd had a lazy morning like this.

She suppressed her own yawn as she stretched out on the sofa just for a couple of minutes. Then she'd do some laundry or prep more jars of baby food. In just a couple of minutes…

Hayes couldn't remember the last time he'd slept during daylight hours—probably not since his hospital stay, bedridden from his injury and pumped full of pain meds. Now, he woke to find himself in the nursery, Mateo still sleeping soundly in his arms. His phone rested on the side table, right where he'd left it after silencing the flood of responses in the family chat, hoping not to wake his son.

Still groggy, he looked through his missed messages. It was mostly everyone chiming in with follow-up questions and Madeline saying that her mom hadn't given her the slightest clue about what the emergency was. There were several messages about a time that worked best for the meeting, but none of those had come from Penn. As usual, his brother was radio silent.

Hayes decided to switch tactics and see if Penn might respond to a group chat message if it didn't involve any drama about their father or his wives. He scrolled through the photos he and Flora had taken earlier today and stared at the first one he'd taken of her with Mateo. It had been so natural, so simple, he couldn't help but capture a candid moment between mother and son. His lungs expanded with every breath as he stared at the photo that made his chest feel fuller. It was too personal to send to his siblings, though, so he scrolled through the rest and paused at the last one with him and Mateo both looking at the camera as they pet Velvet.

He sent the image, and it didn't take long to get a response. In fact, Penn was the first one to reply, even though he only sent a thumbs-up emoji. It was proof that his brother was at least paying attention. Madeline sent a heart and Jillian texted a series of exclamation points. Shelby, who hadn't been with the other two when they'd gone to Flora's store for a not-so-subtle in-person look at their nephew, replied,

Wow, Hayes. I can't believe how much he looks like you. You two definitely won the genetic lottery with those matching blues eyes!

Hayes stared at the simple words on the screen as he tried to recall the color of his own father's eyes. Penn had green eyes, and he was pretty sure none of their sisters had blue eyes. He'd never really paid attention to who looked like who growing up and only remembered an old black-and-white photo of Twinkie and Grandma Morgan on their wedding day. He must take after his mother's side of the family tree.

Mateo stirred in his arms and Hayes enjoyed the next few moments watching his sleepy son slowly awaken.

"You ready to change that diaper?" he asked the baby, who blinked up at him. "And maybe put on a clean shirt that doesn't have half your breakfast down the front?"

Hayes carried Mateo out to the sitting room and saw

Flora sound asleep on the sofa. He stopped in his tracks. The pictures he'd just scrolled through weren't half as beautiful as the woman in real life. He had no idea how long he stood there, watching her chest rise and fall peacefully. With her working full-time and raising their child on her own, he doubted she got to enjoy many naps or even a full night's rest. "Shh. Let's let Mommy sleep, too."

They made their way across the house to the only other space that was familiar to Hayes. The kitchen. Mateo immediately pointed at the bananas on the center island.

Flora had brought the high chair back inside and cleaned it, along with the takeout boxes and plates from breakfast. It was well after lunchtime, so Hayes didn't see any harm in getting another meal ready for his son.

When she padded into the kitchen an hour later, the sink was full and Hayes was in the middle of a video call with his mom who was trying to teach Mateo how to say Gigi.

"Is that Flora?" his mom asked, and the woman in question whipped her head around—her expression shifting from sleepy to shocked. Hayes would've laughed if he wasn't feeling so guilty for the surprise introduction.

Flora stayed on the other side of the center island, so she was out of the video frame, and forcefully shook her head at Hayes. "Mom, I think Flora was hoping to meet you under less…casual circumstances."

"Well, honey, if it makes her feel any better, tell her I have paint splatter in my hair and I'm wearing the Bob Ross T-shirt you and Penn got me for Mother's Day fifteen years ago."

Flora narrowed her eyes and under her breath murmured something that sounded like *I'll get you back* before stepping into the video frame next to Hayes.

"Hi, Mrs. Fortune. It's nice to meet you."

"Please call me Damaris. After all, we're family now." His mother's smile was much more welcoming than it had been a couple of months ago when she'd been introduced to Hayes's other "family" members. "Mateo is the most beautiful baby I've ever seen. I'm so glad that you made me his grandmother."

"Thank *you*?" Flora made it sound like a question.

"Well, she did have a little help from me, Mom," Hayes said, then held the phone closer to Mateo. "Did you see he has my blue eyes?"

"Hmm," was his mom's only reply.

Hayes turned the phone back to him, but it was clear that his mom was distracted by something off in the distance. "Anyway, Mom, I'm glad you can make it out a day early. One of the benefits of having lifetime access to Fortune Air's fleet of private jets, I guess."

"Your father's generosity knows no bounds," she said, not bothering to hide the sarcasm in her voice. "First-class travel arrangements to meet with a woman who has no class."

Taffy was Damaris's least favorite of Archibald's many secrets so, clearly, she wasn't looking forward to whatever the woman had to say tomorrow at the so-called emergency meeting.

"I'm sure it'll be a waste of time. But at least you'll get to meet your grandson sooner."

"That's right." His mom's eyes brightened and she rubbed at a spot of paint on her chin. "Can't wait to see you tomorrow. I hope you both enjoy the rest of your afternoon."

His mother disconnected first, which wasn't really like her. But Hayes needed to talk to Flora anyway now that she was awake. "So, I noticed some red bumps on Mateo when I was changing his diaper earlier. I think it might've been diaper rash, so I used that tube of ointment on the changing table. Do you think we should call the doctor, though?"

"No, the ointment usually takes care of it pretty quickly," she replied. "So, your mom is coming into town tomorrow? Does that have to do with Madeline's mom calling for a family meeting?"

"Yes." Hayes pinched the bridge of his nose. "But the last thing I want to think about right now is that stupid meeting."

"Right." Flora nodded, then surveyed the messy kitchen and asked, "What did you guys have for lunch?"

"Well, Mateo had banana and something orange in a jar and about half a container of those little puff snack things. I tried to make spaghetti, but you can see how that turned out. I'd make sandwiches but you're out of deli meat."

"I was going to go to ER Grocery this afternoon anyway."

"Then let me get Mateo changed and we'll go with you."

"Hayes." She said only his name, but the pointed look she gave him spoke volumes. His stomach dropped knowing that he'd obviously done something to cross the imaginary boundaries she insisted on.

He recovered quickly though by suggesting, "Or you

can go to the store and Mateo and I will stay here and clean the kitchen."

"I'm not worried about the store or the kitchen."

"Then why is there a crease right here?" He used a finger to smooth the frown line between her two eyebrows.

She took a step back and he hoped he hadn't made things worse by touching her so intimately.

"You are in my home every single night. You know where we keep the pasta strainer and how we fold the bath towels and could probably tell me the contents of my medicine cabinet." She picked up a pad of paper. "You even started a grocery list of what's missing from my pantry. Yet, you don't share anything with me about your life. I know you're staying at the hotel, but you haven't exactly said where you live when you're not there. Or even how long you plan to be there. You want me to meet your mom, apparently much sooner than originally planned—and tell me you're tired of secrets—but when it comes to the rest of your family, you're totally close-lipped."

"I'm not purposely keeping things from you, Flora. I'm trying to shield you and Mateo from the drama. All the nonsense."

"That's probably the same thing your father thought when he kept all of his secrets from you guys," she noted.

Her words hit him with a force he hadn't expected and his jaw instinctively tightened. "That's a pretty unfair comparison from someone who didn't even know my father. And someone who kept a pretty big secret of her own."

"You're right." Flora ran a hand through her sleep-tussled hair. "I didn't know your father. I barely know *you.* And, yes, I did keep a pretty big secret from you initially. But I'm trying to rectify that by letting you inside my world. By showing you that I don't have anything to hide. I guess that's my point. I don't like feeling like I'm the only one being vulnerable—the only one who doesn't have a clue about anything that's going on or how things are going to turn out."

Defensiveness left his body and regret replaced the tension. "I assure you that you are not alone in feeling that way."

He took a step toward Flora, intending to apologize for making her feel as though he wasn't willing to let her inside his world. When she tilted her face up toward his, though, he forgot what he was going to say and decided to show her just how vulnerable he felt when it came to her.

His kiss wasn't slow or gentle. It was deep and all-consuming and filled with every ounce of passion he'd been holding back these past few days. Flora responded by wrapping her arms around his neck and pressing her body into his as she met his tongue thrust for thrust.

Hayes lifted her onto the counter behind them and she quickly locked her legs around his waist, drawing him closer. He'd already unbuttoned the top three buttons of her shirt when the sound of their son's giggle came from the high chair.

Flora pulled away first, her cheeks pink, her lips swollen. She shoved a strand of hair behind her ear and cleared her throat before asking, "So what else do we need from the grocery store?"

# *Chapter Eight*

For anyone passing by them at the gourmet market in town, Flora, Hayes and Mateo looked like the quintessential little family out running everyday errands together.

Mateo sat in the shopping cart seat while Hayes pushed him, and Flora wandered the aisles trying to remember what ingredients she would need to make her great-grandmother's *chile verde*.

"Do you want to call her and ask?" he asked when they were standing in front of the spice section for the third time. "It's only fair that I participate in an awkward face time with one of your relatives after you walked in on my call with my mom earlier."

Flora looked at the time on her phone. "No. The new season of *Island Bachelors* came out today and Tita won't answer any calls that aren't a five-alarm emergency. How about tacos? I can probably manage those on my own."

"Please don't feel like you have to cook for me." Hayes wrapped an arm around her waist and softly kissed her forehead. "I wasn't kidding when I said I love greasy spoon diners and eating on the road. I'd just as soon go to Chuck's Chili Wagon for dinner."

"As tempting as that culinary experience might be—" Flora put her hand on his chest "—I'm trying to fit into my prematernity wardrobe and not clog my arteries before I turn thirty."

"I think you look great in whatever wardrobe you want to wear. Or *not* wear." He kissed her again and Mateo giggled.

Their son thought it was hilarious every time they kissed, which had become somewhat of a game this afternoon. Mateo would make a smacking sound with his lips, Hayes would imitate the sound as he gave Flora a soft peck, and then they'd all laugh. The kisses had been much more chaste than the one in the kitchen earlier, but at this rate, Hayes and Flora were no longer waiting for Mateo's prompting to put their lips—or their hands—on each other.

Another shopping cart turned the corner and nearly crashed into them. Flora vaguely recognized the woman as someone from Emerald Ridge, yet it was clear the other shopper knew who Hayes was.

"Oh, hello," the woman managed to get out before taking a shaky breath.

"Agatha," Hayes tipped his head politely. "This is Flora Rodriguez and our son, Mateo. Flora, this is Shelby and Jillian's mother, Agatha."

"It's very nice to meet you." She shook the woman's delicate hand and noticed there was a slight tremble.

"You own the children's boutique, right?" Agatha asked, and Flora nodded. "My daughter Shelby is expecting soon and I've been meaning to stop by and pick up something for the first Fortune..."

The woman trailed off as her eyes landed on Mateo. It was obvious to Flora that Agatha had just realized that her daughter's baby wouldn't be the first one in the next generation of Fortunes.

"Grandbabies are so exciting," Flora said brightly, trying to ease the awkward tension. "Have you picked out your 'grandmother' name yet?"

Agatha blinked back a tear and smiled faintly. "I have a few in mind. Although, I'll probably answer to anything but Mimi. My friend is a Mimi and it gets really confusing not knowing if they're saying Mimi or Mommy."

Mateo made a smacking sound with his lips and Agatha gasped. "Oh, he knows how to blow kisses already!"

Agatha responded by touching her mouth to her fingers and then blowing a kiss back to Mateo. The baby grinned but didn't giggle the same way he would've if he'd gotten the expected response of seeing his parents kiss.

"He really is a cutie," Agatha said. "Those curls of his are so beautiful."

"I wish I had curls like his," Flora agreed, shoving back a straight strand of hair that had escaped her ponytail. "It's going to be a tough day when he gets his first haircut."

Hayes's neck swiveled in her direction. "You already scheduled his first haircut?"

"No." She almost laughed at the stricken look on his face. "But someday he'll have to have one."

"You'll let me know before that happens, right?"

"It's not going to happen anytime soon, Hayes."

"My husband was the same way," Agatha said to Flora in a confiding tone. "Wanted to know every little thing that was going on with our girls. Probably because he had to be away for work so much…"

She trailed off again as she looked at Hayes, realization dawning in her eyes before they filled with tears.

"Please don't cry, Agatha." Hayes surprised Flora, and likely himself, when he immediately wrapped the older woman in a hug. "It's okay for you to hold on to whatever good memories you have of him."

"I'm trying to. But then I'm reminded of the betrayal, and I wish I could go back in time and just… I don't even know what I'd do differently." Agatha finally stepped away from Hayes and dug a tissue out of her purse. "I just want to stop crying all the time."

Flora's heart broke for the woman who was still grieving her husband while being comforted by his son from another marriage.

Perhaps Flora had been too hard on Hayes earlier today when she'd accused him of keeping this part of his life a secret from her. It was complicated and messy and involved so many other people. He was obviously trying to do the right thing for everyone else in his family, while also trying to be a good father to Mateo.

Flora and the baby finished shopping while Hayes got Agatha through the checkout line and out to her car. If she ever wondered what she'd seen in the guy eighteen months ago, it certainly wasn't *this* side of him. He'd been fun and charming and exactly what she'd needed that weekend they'd met. And he still was. But today he was showing her how much she'd underestimated him.

The drive back to her house was quiet.

Hayes had the baby in one arm and three bags of groceries in the other when he turned to Flora in her driveway and said, "You promise that you'll tell me before Mateo gets his first haircut?"

"Of course I'll tell you."

"Because I really want to be there for all the firsts. The first steps, the first words, the first T-ball game, the first time he drives. I mean, obviously, there might be stuff that happens when I'm not there. But I want to know about all the firsts as soon as they happen."

"Then we will do our best to keep you as informed as possible," she said. After all, making sure someone was informed wasn't the same thing as making sure they were *involved.* Once his family issues were resolved and his work obligations took him away from Emerald Ridge, he might not be in a hurry to come back.

"Thank you," he said on an exhale.

Mateo smacked his lips and was rewarded with seeing his parents kiss again.

Chuck's Chili Wagon had been a bad idea last night, Hayes decided as he reached for the roll of antacid tablets on the bedside table in his hotel room.

Yesterday, he and Flora had managed to meet each other halfway on so many different issues, it felt like they'd crossed some sort of emotional bridge together and were well on their way to growing more comfortable around one another. So comfortable, in fact, that all the casual touching and kissing was definitely going to lead to more if they weren't careful. It might've even escalated last night, except Flora had given in to his dinner suggestion and they'd driven to the roadside food truck parked outside of town for a heaping bowlful of chili with onions, cheese and enough spicy peppers to kill any possible foodborne pathogens.

By the time Hayes had gotten Mateo to sleep, Flora was on her second trip to the bathroom in her parents' wing of the house and had sent him a text suggesting he show himself out. She would call him in the morning when she was feeling better. Thankfully, he didn't experience the same symptoms until he made it back to his hotel.

Hayes picked up his phone and sent her a quick text.

I'm feeling much better this morning. How about you?

He saw the three dots appear on his screen as she typed, then read her response.

Much better, but I'm never again letting you talk me into trying something with the words Diablo's Revenge in the description.

Hayes laughed then typed back:

I think it was all the corn bread we ate.

We both know it wasn't the corn bread. Good luck with your family meeting today.

After a hot shower and a few more antacid tablets, Hayes decided to give his stomach a break and skip the coffee this morning. He picked up an icy cold smoothie on his way to the airfield.

While he hadn't expected Penn to actually show up, Hayes had to ignore the lump of disappointment in his throat and smile at his mom as she came down the steps of the smaller Fortune Air jet alone.

Not that this meeting was anything that Penn had to attend. It was more about being there to support their mother. To support *each other.* Growing up, it had always been the three of them. Hayes couldn't think of a tighter trio…other than the triplet attorneys. That was why Penn's absence was all the more baffling. It's not like traveling to Emerald Ridge was a hardship. They had a fleet of private jets at their beck and call. Although, that might change soon if his brother didn't get himself here soon to help the rest of them. Hayes kept that thought to himself as he greeted his mother on the tarmac with a hug and took her suitcase.

"Do you think Taffy found your dad's missing heir yet?" Damaris asked as soon as they were inside his truck.

"Who knows?" he replied truthfully. "Madeline is just as clueless as the rest of us. But I should warn you that Taffy reserved the exact same conference room we'd used when Huey, Louie and Dewey gathered us all together for the first time."

"Will your father's attorneys be there?" Since the reading of the will, his mother had started referring to her late husband only as "your father" when talking to her sons. It was as though she couldn't bear to say the name Archibald or to think of him as the man she'd been married to for almost thirty years.

"Not that I know of." Hayes turned onto the highway that would take them into Emerald Ridge. "So, I doubt it's anything too serious. Although, I ran into Agatha yesterday and she's still taking things pretty hard. So hopefully it's some good news because I don't want to ask the hotel staff for another box of tissues."

"I never leave home without them anymore." His mother pulled a travel-sized pack out of her purse. "I have backup in my suitcase, too."

She turned toward the rolling bag Hayes had put in the back seat and then gasped. "Oh, my word. Would you look at that!"

He used his rearview mirror to see what she was talking about. "Oh. It's for Mateo. Why do you sound so shocked?"

"Because you're the last person I ever expected to see driving around with a car seat." He hadn't seen his mom smile like this in a while and he was glad that his child was the silver lining on the very dark storm cloud that was still hanging over the Fortune family. "Is there a Baby on Board sticker on your back window, too?"

"No. Flora said I don't need one because I drive slower than an old pack mule whenever Mateo is back there."

His mom laughed as he told her about his son and some of the more unexpected moments of fatherhood that Hayes hadn't been ready for. "I know you said I was the last person you'd expect to be a dad, and maybe that used to be the case. But something came over me the moment I saw Mateo for the first time. I don't know what it is, but I can't get enough of him."

"I am so happy for you, Hayes. I know you don't have much experience with kids, but there's never been any doubt in my mind that you'd be an amazing father. You've always been so kind and patient with animals.

Remember that time you brought home that cat because you thought it was a stray?"

"It was always outside and it didn't have a collar or a tag. How was I supposed to know Wilson belonged to the neighbors?"

"Because he weighed over twenty pounds." His mom made a soft snorting sound. "Someone was obviously feeding him."

"Apparently, every other kid on our block thought he was a stray, too, because Penn caught him sneaking treats over at Taylor's house, too. Wilson had no loyalty at all."

"At least your father finally gave in and let you boys get a pet of your own."

"Mom, he gave me twenty bucks to buy a turtle from the pet store."

She shifted in her seat to face him. "I thought you loved Fast Eddie."

"Yeah, he was great. For a turtle. Meanwhile, Dad's other kids had a stable full of horses."

"True. But I'm sure your father's daughters can think of some things they wished for that you boys got instead."

"I'll tell you what." Hayes reached across the console and squeezed her hand. "Penn and I definitely got the best mom."

Damaris smiled, but the overall mood in the cab of the truck slowly shifted as they approached the hotel. By the time he pulled into a parking spot, his mom was nervously wringing her hands together.

Helping her out of the truck, Hayes put a reassuring arm around her shoulder, noticing she'd gotten thinner and he could feel the outline of her bone under her light sweater. "It'll be fine, Mom. Let's get you checked into your room first so you can get refreshed before we meet everyone else."

Thirty minutes later, Hayes walked his mother into the conference room where his sisters and Agatha were already waiting. The wasted space of such a large meeting area was even more unnecessary without Penn and the attorneys there. Despite having such a vast emptiness surrounding them, the air seemed to leave the room when Taffy Fortune made her grand entrance a few minutes later.

Agatha made a sniffling sound and Damaris twisted her fingers in her lap as Archibald Fortune's third wife went straight to the head of the long conference table and set a leather portfolio on the glass top with such a theatrical flourish, the corner of a reprinted newspaper clipping slipped out.

"You're being very dramatic, Mom," Madeline said through a forced smile. "Is all of this really necessary?"

"Oh, I think it's *very* necessary." Taffy was possibly younger than the other two wives. Her bleached blonde hair and heavily mascaraed eyes were quite the contrast to Agatha, a demure brunette with classic looks, and to Hayes's mom, whose auburn hair was usually styled in sophisticated waves—except when she tied it up in a colorful scarf to keep it out of her paint palette. "Since Archie's four children haven't seemed to have much luck getting any answers, I've decided to hire my own private investigator."

Hayes's eyes narrowed at the woman's calculated use of the word *children* when referring to him and his sisters. It also wasn't lost on him that she'd purposely excluded Penn from her count.

"Five," he bit out, correcting her.

Taffy put a manicured hand to her ear and said, "What's that?"

"I said there's five of us." Hayes used the most convincing tone he could, hoping his brother didn't make a liar out of him. "Even though Penn isn't here right now, he will be eventually."

"Wrong," Taffy said a bit too gleefully. "I was already counting Penn when I said Archie's *four* children."

Hayes heard a whimpering sound that might've come from his mom, but it was Agatha who cried out, "Oh for heaven's sake, Taffy. I can't take any more of this."

"Agatha's right, Mom," Madeline chided. "We've all been through enough already. Stop playing word games and just come out and say whatever it is that was so important you had to drag all of us here."

"Like I was saying…" Taffy who was the only one in the room still standing, put her crimson tipped fingernails on the tabletop and leaned forward. "I hired my own investigator to do some research. Not just on the missing heir, but on all of you."

"That's pretty intrusive," either Shelby or Jillian mumbled.

Hayes couldn't tell which sister had said it, though, because he'd followed Taffy's calculated gaze to his mother's face, which had gone completely pale.

"Imagine my surprise when my PI sent me a very interesting newspaper article depicting you in particular, Damaris. I believe it was at the opening of some gallery in Paris. It's in French, of course, but the photo of you cozied up with the artist doesn't require any translation." Taffy's words sent a chill down Hayes's spine.

He was so focused on his mom's stricken expression, he barely heard Taffy add, "Do you want to air your dirty laundry or shall I?"

"Mom?" Hayes shifted his face in front of her, trying to block Taffy from her view. When his mother's wide eyes finally met his gaze, he quietly asked, "Are you okay?"

All he cared about right that second was protecting his mother. He'd process the implication of Taffy's accusation later.

Damaris blinked, then drew a deep breath, releasing it with a shudder. Whether she was wearing a paint-splattered T-shirt or a tailored suit like the one she'd changed into today, his educated and elegant mother had always been the epitome of a class act. So even though she was clearly shaken, she slowly rose to her feet and said to nobody in particular, "If you'll excuse us, I'd like to speak with my son privately."

Hayes didn't so much as look in anyone else's direction as he followed his mother out of the conference room. He was by her side and linked her arm through his before the door closed behind them. She nearly collapsed against him, her legs were so unsteady.

"Let's find a place to sit down," he said as he steered her toward a quiet alcove near the lobby. Once he got her situated on a small sofa, he took the overstuffed chair beside her. "Should I go get us a drink?"

His mother shook her head, but she did reach for her purse and pulled out her pack of tissues. Tears had finally formed in her eyes and Hayes nearly sagged in relief. He could handle tears much better than the frozen panic he'd seen on her face a few minutes ago.

He waited a few more moments for his mom to get her thoughts together, then asked, "Do you know what Taffy was talking about back there?"

"Unfortunately, I do. And it was something I had never wanted you to hear."

Hayes's heart began to pound and the words *Archie's four children* began replaying in his head. "Just tell me, Mom."

"You have to understand that I was very lonely in my marriage to your father. I'm not proud of what I did and I'm certainly not making excuses. But one time, after Penn was born, I considered leaving him because I didn't think I could stay married to someone who loved his company more than he loved me." Her voice cracked and she swallowed hard. "He begged me not to divorce him, which in hindsight, makes me think that he was more concerned about me finding out our marriage wasn't legal than actually losing me."

Hayes hadn't wanted to look into the legal ramifications of his father's betrayal to his multiple wives, so he'd told himself to trust the attorneys and only focus on finding the missing sibling. As far as he was concerned, his parents had loved each other at one time and had decided to have a family together. The titles of husband and wife were just that…titles.

"Your father and I agreed to a trial separation for a month," his mother continued. "He thought I was suffering from some sort of delayed postpartum depression after having Penn. Your brother was already a year old, so I knew it wasn't that. But your father insisted I needed a break, a long vacation, and then I'd be all better. My parents hired a nanny to take care of Penn at their home, and I went to France to find myself. It was a whirlwind four weeks and I was surrounded by beautiful art and charming men who were paying attention to me, men who saw me as a passionate woman with needs, men who wanted to paint me in the nu—"

"I get it!" Hayes held up his palm. "You can skip that part, Mom."

"Like I was saying, France had everything I thought I was missing living in Texas. Everything except Penn, that is. But I knew he was in good hands and I told myself that by recharging my emotional battery, I would be coming back to him as a happier, refreshed mom."

A wistful look crossed her features, her eyes distant for a moment, as if recalling a bittersweet memory.

"And France was *intoxicating*, just like it had been when I was studying abroad in college. I felt young again. I felt free. I wasn't the least bit lonely. I met a group of art students, and we spent a weekend in the French Riveria. And let me tell you, I had never felt so free and so uninhibited, basking in the sun on those topless beaches—"

She paused long enough to make a tsking sound. "Stop scrunching your face like that, Hayes. Anyway, I met a man, and we had a brief fling. I figured that your father and I were separated, so it wasn't cheating, technically. Certainly not as bad as what he was apparently doing back home." She sighed. "But I digress. Your father flew out to Paris and was waiting for me at the hotel. He said he missed me and couldn't live without me. He spent the week following me to art museums, eating at sidewalk cafés and pulling out all the stops to win me back. And it worked. I flew back to Texas with him and when my parents brought Penn to me, I was so happy to have my baby in my arms again. My life made sense again. Two months later, I found out I was pregnant with you."

"So, what Taffy said was true. I'm not Archibald Fortune's son."

He hadn't bothered framing it as a question. Just hearing the words come out of his own mouth filled Hayes with shame. It made him feel like a complete fraud, even though he hadn't done anything wrong. He wanted to bury his head in his hands, but he also needed to see his mom's face when she confirmed that his entire existence was based on a lie.

"The truth is that I don't know. With the timing of everything, I can't be sure." His mom reached for his hand and gave him an imploring look. "I know that's not very reassuring, but Archibald was your father in every way that mattered. He was there when you were born and he loved you, even when he couldn't be with us as often as we wanted him to be. He was a smart man and while he and I never talked about my time in France, he could've asked questions. He could've done his own digging and would've easily found out. The newspaper that published the photo Taffy's PI found was pretty well circulated back then. But I don't think your father cared whether you were biologically his or not."

"How could he *not* have cared?" Hayes rasped, thinking about his own son. The second he'd laid eyes on Mateo, the bond was instinctive. It was *immediate*. And it wasn't just because they looked so much alike. "Do you know that I'm the only one of his children…or should I say heirs…who has blue eyes?"

His mom nodded slowly. "I noticed that. But you know what? Your father loved your blue eyes. He hated it when

I went through that black-and-white photography phase and complained that he couldn't see the vibrant blue of your eyes in those pictures."

Maybe Archibald was obsessed with eye color because it reminded him that Hayes might not be his son. But it seemed like an unnecessary and hurtful thing to point out to Damaris. Instead, Hayes asked, "Did the other guy have blue eyes?"

"No." His mother said simply, "I have no idea how you ended up with them or why your father made such a big deal out of it."

The shame that had been filling him earlier was slowly coiling into a ball in the pit of his stomach. "It sounds weird to hear you calling him my father when he might not be."

"As far as I'm concerned, and as far as *he* was concerned, Archibald Fortune is your father. No matter what Taffy's useless PI says."

"But how do you know, Mom? How can you be sure of anything when it comes to that man? His entire life was nothing but lies. Do you know that he grew up here in Emerald Ridge? That his parents didn't die until he was fourteen? And who knows what else we'll discover when we figure out the key to his secret property. Or should I say when *they* figure it out. His real heirs."

His mom reached over and cupped his chin in her palm, just like she used to when he was a little boy and she wanted him to pay attention to what she was about to say.

"His love for you and your brother was never a lie, Hayes. Nor was his love for me. I can't speak to his relationships with his other families, and I'm certainly not trying to defend the choices that he made. But Archibald Fortune was wealthy and powerful and driven, and he didn't do a damn thing unless he wanted to. He wanted our family. He wanted you."

"Or maybe he just had to accept me because he didn't want to lose *you*," Hayes challenged. "The man could barely stand to lose a board game on those rare occasions he blessed us with his presence. He clearly didn't like the idea of divorce."

"Let me ask you this." His mother sat up straighter. "When you go to Flora's house every night, is it because you want to be with her or because you want to be with your son?"

"It's because I want to spend time with my son," Hayes said immediately. Although, he certainly enjoyed Flora's company, as well. In fact, more than he cared to admit. "But my situation is unique."

"Right," his mom said. "Everyone thinks their situation is unique. That doesn't mean it's any more special or any more difficult. It just means that it's yours and you know it better than anyone else. All you can hope is that, one day, someone doesn't come along and try to tell your son that his father didn't love him. Your dad may not have always shown it, but he loved you unconditionally." Her eyes softened, still glistening with tears as she searched his face for understanding. "He isn't here anymore to tell you himself and I can't blame you for not trusting me right now, Hayes. But I sure as hell hope that if your son ever finds himself in a similar position as you're in now, he can listen to reason and not to some two-bit, vindictive snake with a bad bleach job and an axe to grind."

He blinked his eyes several times, shocked to hear his normally poised mother speak so ill of someone. Although, that should be less of a surprise than her talking about the topless beaches and the nude art model thing. Hayes shuddered and pushed that out of his mind.

The problem was that Hayes didn't feel as though he could trust anyone about *anything* at this point. But he also wasn't going to judge his mother for a fling that may or may not have resulted in a pregnancy when he'd also had a child following his own romantic weekend. Granted, neither Hayes nor Flora were married to other people at the time.

He took his mother's hand, the one that had just cupped his face earlier. "I love you, Mom. No matter what. But it's going to take some time for everything to sink in."

"I love you, too. And I'm so sorry that I didn't tell you…" She shivered. "Honestly, there would probably never have been a good time to tell you. But I'm sorry that you had to find out the way you did."

"It's been a rough morning, and I don't see the point in you going back into that conference room to listen to more of Taffy's wild speculations and accusations. You take some time for yourself, and I'll go explain things to everyone."

Hayes rose, as well. "There's no way I'm letting you go back into that room alone. I know you want to protect me, but someone needs to protect you, too."

His mom took a deep breath, then extended her hand so that he could help her rise from the sofa.

"By the way, don't be surprised when she asks you to get a DNA test."

*"Asks?"* Hayes chuckled, but there was nothing funny about the situation. "Taffy doesn't ask for things. She demands. But at this point, I'd like a DNA test, as well. All of that can wait, though. I'll walk you to your room before they come out here looking for us. You can call the attorney—or all three of them—if you want, and see how this might affect the terms of the will. I'm going to call Penn before he finds out about this in the group chat."

To be on the safe side, Hayes sent a text to Shelby, Jillian and Madeline—it suddenly felt strange to not think of them collectively as "the sisters"—to let them know that he and his mom weren't coming back to Taffy's meeting. They needed some time to themselves to process everything. He'd reach out later and they could fill him in on anything else he needed to know. He was tempted to add that he didn't want any of them to judge his mother for something that had happened so long ago. But even if they ended up not being his biological sisters, Hayes had gotten to know them well enough by now. They weren't the types who would judge.

Walking his mother to the elevators, Hayes couldn't keep his mind from making comparisons between this new development to his own situation with Flora and Mateo. He pushed the button for Damaris's floor, then asked, "Did you ever let the other guy in France know that he might have a son?"

"No. He died in a boating accident a few months after I returned to the States."

"Would you have?" He suddenly needed to know. "If you'd found out for certain that I was his."

"I know what you're thinking, Hayes." His mother squeezed his hand. "Remember what I said about everyone's situation being unique. Don't dwell on how things could've happened differently between you and Flora. You have a son, and you love him. Nothing else in the past is going to change how you feel about him. And in the future, whether or not he feels your love depends on how much you show it to him every day from here on out. And here's another bit of advice…the same is true of his mother."

# *Chapter Nine*

Hayes left his mom at the door to her room and went to his own. He'd spent so much of the past ten years on the road, traveling from hotel room to hotel room, depending on which rodeo had the biggest purse. His mom had kept things the same back home at first. Eventually, though, she'd decided she needed some changes to her empty nest. One Thanksgiving, he'd come home to see that his childhood bedroom had been redecorated and blended in with every other place he'd visited.

Since then, no place he'd stayed had really felt permanent. Yet, for some reason, being at the Rodriguez house made him feel as though he might eventually want to put down roots. He nearly laughed at how crazy that sounded considering it wasn't even Flora's home. It belonged to her parents.

All he knew was that he'd much rather be there right now than inside his lonely suite at the Emerald Ridge Hotel. They hadn't made plans for today and, for all Hayes knew, she needed a break from him. Less than a week ago, he'd shown up out of the blue and had turned her whole world upside down. If she wanted him to come over tonight to spend time with Mateo, then she could be the one to reach out first this time.

He glanced at his phone and saw three text messages. Shelby told him to take all the time he needed. Jillian said she'd bring the beer and/or wine whenever he was ready to talk. And Madeline apologized for her mother's callous behavior.

While he appreciated their attempts to be supportive, he really didn't feel like talking to anyone with the last name Fortune right now. He sat on the foot of his bed and let himself fall onto his back. He stared at the ceiling for several moments before finally giving in and sending Flora a text.

Can I bring over dinner later?

Her response was immediate.

No

Disappointment flooded him and he squeezed his eyes shut, wishing he hadn't gotten his hopes up after the devastating blow he'd just endured downstairs.

But then his phone buzzed again with a second message from her.

You said I could pick dinner this time and I pick pizza. Mateo and I should be home by 5. Let me know when you're on your way and I'll place an order for delivery.

He had no business being this excited. Especially after the morning he'd just had. But when he was with Flora and his son, Hayes didn't have to think about any of the other drama in his life. It was the same way he got when he climbed onto the back of a horse. He might not know which direction he'd be turning in next, but for that short period of time, he could put all of his focus and energy into something he loved.

Sitting up, he thought about going for a ride this afternoon to clear his head. There was the Fortune's Gold Guest Ranch and Spa, where guests could pay to go for a horseback ride. But he wanted to saddle a horse that wasn't better suited for wannabe cowboys on vacation. Fortune and Daughters Ranch had some pretty impressive Arabians, but he was trying to avoid thinking about what had happened in the conference room earlier today. That would be impossible to do if Agatha started crying again when he drove up to her ranch.

He was about to conduct an online search when his phone rang and he saw his brother's name flash across the screen. Hayes wasn't looking forward to giving Penn an update, but it needed to come from him.

"You missed an eventful meeting," Hayes said by way of greeting.

"Yeah, I thought something might be up. Mom's phone is going straight to voicemail and nobody is saying anything in the family group chat."

"Well, normally you're the one not saying anything in the group chat." Hayes didn't bother keeping the frustration from his voice. Or the pettiness. "So now you know how the rest of us feel."

"Noted. So, what did I miss?"

"Apparently, Mom slept with another man while she was married to Dad, and I might not be a Fortune after all."

Penn didn't respond right away. After a long stretch of

silence, he finally spoke. "So Mom told everyone about the guy in France?"

"No, Taffy did. I guess she hired a private investigator to do background searches on all of us. *Wait*. You already know about the guy in France?"

"Why do you think I've been refusing to come out there and help you guys dig into everyone's past? I told you something like this would happen..."

"Except I thought you were talking about digging up dirt on *Dad*." Confusion ricochet in Hayes's head and he rubbed his temples to help clear it. "This was a secret about Mom. And I guess about me. How long have you known about this? And more importantly, why didn't you tell me?"

"About the French guy? I overheard Mom talking to Aunt Diana about it a long time ago. I was in high school."

"You overheard our mother telling her sister that she had an affair and I might not be Dad's son, yet you never bothered to share that with me?" What else had his brother known about that he kept hidden?

"I was a dumb teenager at the time, Hayes. My decision-making skills weren't as finely honed back then. Plus, you were always talking bad about Dad for having to leave town to work. I didn't want you to hold a grudge against Mom, too."

"So, you've had over ten years to tell me and never did?" he seethed, his voice vibrating with anger.

"To be honest with you, I was more focused on the fact that Mom and Dad's marriage was a sham. I never even thought about the possibility that she could've gotten pregnant during her affair. The only part of the conversation I heard was Aunt Diana telling Mom that she shouldn't put up with Dad being gone all the time and that she wished Mom would've spent more time with some dude in France instead of letting Dad talk her into coming back home." Penn blew out a rough breath. "Your name didn't even come up in that conversation. It wasn't until Dad died and I started doing the math in my head that I realized it might be best if nobody has any reason to question your parentage."

Hayes tried not to lash out but failed. "Did you ever think that maybe you should've given me the heads-up that it might become an issue?"

"I thought about it for a few minutes. But you were so pissed at Dad by that point and you two had never really gotten along that well. I knew that you might be looking for any reason to cut your losses and distance yourself from the whole mess." Penn cleared this throat. "And to be honest with you, man, I was trying to wrap my head around the fact that I had all these half siblings I knew nothing about. Selfishly, I didn't want to admit that the only full sibling I have, the only one who was raised in the same house as me, might not be my brother after all."

Hayes's fingers clenched before he extended them completely open. He had never wanted to punch someone harder or hug someone tighter than he wanted to right now.

"I'm still your brother, Penn. No matter who my dad ends up being. Nothing is going to change the fact that we grew up together and shared everything we had with each other."

"I know that. *Logically.*" Penn paused and Hayes didn't need to use his imagination to see the same pain and frustration reflected in his brother's eyes. They'd both been lied to by their parents. But Hayes had the added upset of being the last to know. "So, how's Mom doing now that everyone knows?"

He told Penn about leaving the meeting early with their mother and getting the full story from her. "And when I say *full story*, I mean you owe me big-time for having to hear our mother talk about topless beaches and all the men who saw her as a passionate woman with needs."

"Eww. But try being a teenager and overhearing Aunt Diana asking Mom about upper lip waxing."

"Not the same, partner. You could've left whatever room you were eavesdropping in if you didn't want to hear that," Hayes pointed out.

"First of all, I wasn't eavesdropping. We were at Grandma Morgan's beach house for Fourth of July, and I was in the broom closet looking for those firecrackers Uncle Kevin caught us with and took away. Aunt Diana and Mom came into the kitchen and started talking. Second of all, I *did* leave. Right through that small window with the broken screen, and onto the back porch. And third of all? Forget all of that. I want to know what happened to Mom after the two of you had your big talk away from everyone else?"

He rubbed the back of his neck, his jaw still tight. "I told Mom there was no point in going back to the conference room to watch Taffy gloat. I walked her back to her room and she said she was going to call the attorney."

"I guess we have to wait and find out what happens next?"

"I'm not going to wait," Hayes said. "I'm going to get a DNA test."

Penn groaned. "This is such a damn mess."

"You're right it is," Hayes told his brother. "And now there's even more of a reason for you to get out here and help fix it."

Flora could tell from the look on Hayes's face that his family meeting hadn't gone well. But he still smiled at Mateo, handling the feeding and bath time with even more tenderness and care than usual. If that was possible. Hayes had told her that he wanted to be more present than his own father had been, but that could've simply meant he wanted to be there for the fun stuff. She hadn't expected him to take such an active role, though. His paternal instincts continued to surprise her.

At first, she'd found reasons to hover when Hayes insisted on taking over many of the same tasks that she'd done the past nine months as Mateo's primary caretaker. How could she not? When someone tells you they've never so much as pushed a baby stroller, it's hard not to stand there and watch the first time to make sure they're doing it right. However, it didn't take long for Hayes to prove himself to be more than capable with their son, giving Flora no reason to doubt that Mateo was in good hands.

The only thing she still doubted was that Hayes wouldn't get sick of playing daddy eventually. Or, judging by the tired circles under his eyes and the lack of playfulness in his normally upbeat voice, he'd become overwhelmed and overburdened by everything else in his life. He was a cowboy without a horse or ranch or any other familiar outlet to ease his stress. The man was still staying in a hotel that he could check out of on any given day.

When he walked out of Mateo's quiet nursery, Flora was waiting for him in the small sitting area she'd converted to a living room. She held up a bottle of wine and two glasses. "You look like you could use a drink."

"What I could really use is a good horse and a long ride out in the fresh country air. Or some backbreaking, mind-numbing labor in the stables. And *then* a drink."

It was as though he was giving voice to her earlier thoughts. He needed more than what he'd found so far in Emerald Ridge. All she could offer him was a listening ear.

"Well, I don't have a horse or stables, but I can provide some fresh country air if you want to grab the baby monitor and follow me."

She tucked the bottle under her arm and grabbed a throw blanket off the sofa before leading him to the back patio. The sun had just set, but the sky was still dusk-colored and the air still had traces of the earlier warmth of the day.

"I can see him on the screen, but I can't tell if his music is already done playing." Hayes fiddled with the volume on the baby monitor. "Are you sure this will work out here?"

"Positive," she said passing him the blanket. He spread it out on the grass and then took the glasses from her so she could open the bottle and pour the wine.

It would've looked like a picture-perfect setting for romance, except there was clearly something weighing heavily on Hayes's broad shoulders. Flora wanted to ask what had happened, but she also knew that he'd tell her when he was ready. As long as he didn't think his problems would burden her.

She thought about asking him about his camps and telling him she'd gone on the website to learn more about what he did. However, she wasn't sure how to go about that without bringing up the subject of rodeos, a topic that they still tried to avoid whenever possible.

If it wasn't for the hot kiss they'd had in the kitchen yesterday, she'd be wondering if the only thing they had in common was Mateo. Not that they needed to talk about anything other than their son in order to co-parent. Or to make out. Maybe it was better to keep it that way when they were together. Flora was about to tell him about an upcoming wellness appointment with the pediatrician when Hayes leaned back on his elbows and started speaking.

"I promised myself that I wouldn't add to your already full plate by bringing all of my family drama over here. But something came up today about my heritage—or rather my *potential* heritage—that could potentially affect Mateo. Maybe."

"When you say 'heritage,' do you mean your family background? Or do you mean your inheritance? Because I don't think our son is going to care how much money either of his parents have in the bank as long as we love him."

"I mean all the above. Of course, nobody brought up the word 'inheritance' yet. But I have a feeling that's going to be why the subject came up in the first place." His heavy sigh came out as a half groan, then he downed half the contents in his glass. "It turns out, I may not be a Fortune at all."

"Wow." Her eyes widened. "I guess the emergency meeting was a bigger deal than expected."

They went through the entire bottle of wine as Hayes told her about his mom's affair—which Flora didn't think sounded like a true affair since his parents were technically separated at the time. About Taffy hiring a private investigator to do a background check on all of them—which made Flora think that any woman who'd go to that much trouble to dig up dirt on people definitely intended to benefit from her discovery. And about Penn not telling his brother that their father might not, in fact, be Hayes's father—which Flora knew better than to form an opinion on since she'd also kept important information from Hayes.

Mostly, she just sat there and listened, nodding while letting him get everything off his chest. A rustling sound crackled from the baby monitor and even though the image on the screen showed Mateo sleeping peacefully, Hayes went inside to double-check while Flora headed to the kitchen to get the pizza they'd barely touched earlier and a second bottle of wine.

"The entire time I was feeding and bathing Mateo tonight," Hayes said when he met Flora back outside on the blanket, "I kept staring at his eyes. Do you know that he and I are the only ones in my family with that blue color?"

"I'm the only one in my family whose second toe is longer than their big toe." Flora wasn't trying to be dismissive, however, she didn't see a point in allowing him to go down a rabbit hole of possibilities for some things that couldn't be explained. "Genetics can be very simple, *and* it can be very complicated."

"I never noticed your second toe is bigger." Hayes moved to the lower part of the blanket and leaned forward to study her bare foot. "You're right. It is."

A flush rising to her cheeks, she resisted the urge to tuck her feet under legs to prevent further analyzation. After all, she'd been the one who'd pointed out the toe thing in the first place. Thank goodness Flora had gotten a pedicure recently.

Hayes immediately pulled off his own boots and socks and wiggled his toes above the grass. "Does Mateo have your feet or mine? I never gave it a thought until now."

"Neither have I. My point, Hayes, is that it doesn't matter that some kids have blue eyes and some kids have long toes. If Mateo didn't look so much like you, would it make you love him any less?"

He flinched. "Of course not."

"Don't you think your father felt the same way about you?"

"Who knows how he felt?" Hayes tried to shrug casually, yet it wasn't convincing. "My mom insists that he loved me, but it's kind of hard to feel loved when he was rarely there."

"He obviously loved you enough to never question the possibility that you might not be his. If someone like Taffy could've quickly found out about a weekend fling your mom had in a foreign country nearly thirty years ago, don't you think a man as powerful and well connected as Archibald Fortune could've found out just easily?"

"My mom made a similar point. But we're also talking about a man who wasn't able to find a child he had with his mistress and now has to force his other children to work together to find his missing offspring."

Because she didn't know Archibald or his reasons for forcing his children to come together to work on a task he had been better equipped to handle when he was alive, Flora gave a noncommittal, "Hmm."

Somehow, one of her bare feet had ended up in Hayes's lap and he was massaging it, although his focus seemed somewhere else as he stared off in the distance. His fingers felt so incredible, Flora didn't pull away.

"So, are they making you get a DNA test?" she asked curiously.

"Whether I need to or not, I'm planning to get one for my own peace of mind. I did get an email from our attorney this afternoon, though. My mom called him after the meeting. He said that my father's will isn't clear on the issue of inheritance. Archibald listed us by name as his children, but then he also has a clause in there about the missing heir being confirmed by DNA. That means that if Taffy—or anyone else—wanted to challenge the terms of the will in court, they could possibly have a valid argument."

Flora had only interacted with his half sisters briefly, but they hadn't seemed like the types to want to drag their family name through the mud in a drawn-out court battle. Although, who knew what folks would do when that much money was on the line? She certainly wasn't going to risk steering the conversation in a direction that would have him questioning anyone's loyalty.

"I can understand your reasons for wanting to take the DNA test," she said, knowing that she might possibly regret the next words out of her mouth. "If you want Mateo to have a test, as well, I don't have a problem with that."

"Do *you* want Mateo to have a test?" he asked. "No, don't answer that. Because he's not getting one."

There was never any doubt in Flora's mind about Hayes being the father of her child since she knew there wasn't anyone else it could be. But she hoped his vote of confidence came from trusting her and his instincts rather than wanting to prove to himself that he was different from his own father.

"Sorry, Flora. I know it sounds presumptuous of me to tell you what test our child can and can't get. I have no idea why I'm so upset about finding out that Archibald Fortune might not be my father. I didn't even like the man."

"Were things that bad between the two of you?" she asked softly.

"They weren't *bad*. I mean he wasn't a bad person… well, other than having multiple wives and secret children and all the lies he told." When he said it like that, with a sarcastic tone, it was clear that he was using humor as a defense mechanism. "But it's not like I had a bad childhood or anything. Financially, he took care of us, and my mom always made sure we felt loved. It's just that my dad never made any of us a priority and it was easy for my adolescent brain to interpret that as him not giving a shit about us."

"You can be angry at him and still love him, Hayes. Of course, it hurts. Of course, you're disappointed that he didn't live up to the expectations you had of what a father should be. You need to give yourself permission to feel all of it—the love, the frustration, even the resentment. There'd be something wrong if you *didn't* feel that way."

"Why is it that the only time I don't feel like there's something wrong is when I'm with you?" His hand had traveled from her foot to her calf and was now at her knee.

"Probably the same reason why everything with Mateo goes so much more smoothly for me when you're here." She wasn't sure how her leg had gotten to the other side of him, but all it would take was a slight lift of her hips and she would be on his lap. "There's this connection between us that I can't explain. It's been there since the first time we met. I guess we just work well together."

"Flora." Hayes's hand moved to her waist and easily shifted her entire body so that she was completely facing him, her knees on either side of his hips. "There's something I need to tell you."

"What's that?" she whispered, her face inches from his as his powerful hands spanned the small of her back.

"You know yesterday, when Mateo was doing that lip smacking thing?" he started, his thumbs tracing under her rib cage, teasing her into arching her back until her breasts pressed forward.

"Uh-huh?" she asked. Her hands balanced on his shoulders for support while she tried to concentration on his words and not all of the physical sensations building inside of her.

"I might've been working with him on that trick during bath time because I wanted an excuse to be able to keep kissing you."

She threw back her head and laughed. The rest of her, though, remained firmly in place as he held her against him. Instinctively, her body craved the warmth of his and the intimacy of her chest pressed firmly against his.

"There's something I should tell you, too," she said, her voice just as throaty as his. Ever so slightly, she rocked herself against the fly of his jeans and she heard his the hiss of his indrawn breath.

"What's that?" he whispered, his breath soft and warm on her lips.

"I knew what you were up to the whole time. And I liked it."

He groaned as his mouth moved over hers, setting off the storm that had been brewing between them since the day he'd walked into her store.

She was breathless, practically panting, when his soft lips pressed a trail of kisses to her ear. "If you don't want me to carry you straight to your bed right now, then tell me to leave."

"You know I'm not going to tell you to leave," she rasped. "But you don't have to carry me anywhere, because I'm already on my way there."

She used the element of surprise to jump off his lap and start running toward the house. But Hayes was fast and he was agile. He caught up to her in the enormous living room, right in front of the very formal, very plush, sofa.

They didn't make it to her bed until much much later.

## *Chapter Ten*

Hayes woke up in Flora's room, her warm body curled against his and her dark hair fanned across the pillow beside him. Last night hadn't only been a reminder of the intense sexual chemistry they'd shared eighteen months ago, it had been even more confirmation that when something felt right, neither one of them were afraid of chasing that feeling.

His satisfied grin was interrupted by a staticky sound and he eased away from her so that he could check the baby monitor. After switching off the device so it didn't wake her, he padded into Mateo's room to see his son sitting up in his crib, chewing on the black Stetson like it was his favorite stuffed animal.

Mateo's eyes immediately lit up and he dropped the hat and lifted his chubby arms in the air, babbling happily. "Shh, partner. Your mama is still sleeping. You want to help me make her some breakfast?"

What started off as an idyllic morning, though, soon turned to annoyance as reality set in. Or, rather, the pinging sound of Taffy's demanding text messages forced Hayes to face reality. They came in rapid-fire succession. One right after another as she didn't bother waiting for him to respond.

Here's the name of the lab where I arranged for you to get a DNA test.

Your appointment is on Tuesday at 8:00am sharp.

Don't be late.

I've instructed the lab not to make any changes to the appointment time without my authorization.

It was one thing for Taffy to have the audacity to schedule the time and place for Hayes's DNA test. But why in the hell would the lab need to consult Taffy about an appointment involving *his* schedule?

They will require a valid form of identification.

I will be there to ensure that there are no errors, either accidental or intentional.

Hayes's seriously hoped the woman wasn't insinuating what it sounded like. He finally typed a reply.

Please explain to me how your presence will in any way change the outcome of the test result.

Three blinking dots and then:

I can confirm your identity and that you're the person they're supposed to be testing.

He typed.

The lab staff can confirm who I am with the valid form of identification I'm supposed to bring.

People can make fake IDs and then send in someone else to take the test for them. I've already sent them a picture of Penn so they know not to test him 'by mistake.'

*By mistake* clearly suggested that Hayes might attempt to enlist his brother in committing some sort of fraud by switching places.

"This woman has completely lost her mind," Hayes grumbled to his son as he wiped Mateo's face and lifted him from the high chair.

He then balanced the baby on his hip as he fired off another response to Taffy.

If my goal is to prove that I have the same DNA as Archibald Fortune, then who else would I have show up at the lab to take the test for me? The missing heir that none of us can seem to find?

Her response was to send a link to the lab's website, along with the address and a text restating the appointment date and time.

Nope. Hayes was not going to play this game. In fact, there was no reason for Taffy Fortune to ever message him directly without including other family members—or the attorneys—on the text thread. After taking a screenshot of their exchange, he forwarded it to Madeline, intending to add a message of his own. One that made it clear he had no intention of following Taffy's obsessively controlling orders. If and when he decided to take a DNA test, it would be on his terms and at a location of his choosing.

Before he could type it out, though, his son needed a diaper change and then several other things required Hayes's attention for the next thirty minutes—including kissing Flora good morning when he and a freshly dressed Mateo took her a cup of coffee in bed.

"Be careful." She smiled at him. "I might get used to being spoiled like this."

"After the way you took care of me last night, it would be my pleasure to spoil—" his phone vibrated in his pocket. "Hold on. I have to tell my father's third wife that she can lose my number."

But instead of the notification on his screen showing Taffy's name, it displayed Penn's. He opened his messages and realized that the screen shot he thought he'd sent Madeline had actually gone out in the sibling group chat. His brother had responded, "Check your emails."

"Let me take him," Flora said, reaching for Mateo, "so you can take care of that."

Normally, Hayes wanted to prove that he could multitask with a baby in his arms just as well as Flora could. But he'd already missed that mark when he'd inadvertently sent a group text earlier. Besides, he had a feeling he was going to need to sit down for whatever his brother had deemed serious enough to put in written form.

The first thing he noticed was that Penn had cc'd all of the siblings, their mothers and the attorneys. The second thing was that it was addressed to Taffy specifically.

Dear Taffy,

Please be advised that I will not tolerate you expecting Hayes, or any of my other siblings, to fall in line with your unreasonable and controlling demands. If you want to be mad at our father, then you will need to find a way to direct that anger at the powers that be and not take it out on his children who never asked to be put in this situation. Our father did not name you as executor of his will and, therefore, you are not calling the shots.

If, upon legal counsel, anyone decides to take a DNA test, they will do so at a time and location convenient for them, not you.

Penn

Hayes had known that his sibling would eventually come around and finally interact with the others. But he hadn't expected it to happen in such a firm and commanding way that left no argument about Penn's intention to continue sitting on the sidelines.

His inbox notification indicated another new email and Hayes wasn't surprised to see Taffy had responded so quickly.

How will we know that the DNA test has been done legitimately? Or that Hayes won't lie about the results? I've already arranged for my lab to send the results directly to me.

"Is everything okay?" Flora set Mateo on the carpet so he could practice getting into his crawling position. "I mean I know it's probably not okay, otherwise you wouldn't have that vein popping out on your normally smooth forehead. What I meant to ask is whether there's anything I can do to help."

He huffed out a frustrated breath. "You can explain to me how my father could've been married to someone as sweet as Agatha, to someone as talented as my mom, and yet still end up with someone as callous as Taffy."

Hayes passed Flora his phone so that she could read everything herself while he rubbed the throbbing spot on his forehead.

"It looks like some new emails just came in." She passed the phone back to Hayes.

Penn wrote: Hayes and my mother have the right to find out the results first.

Madeline wrote: Mom, you are going too far.

Shelby wrote: I agree with Penn. And with Madeline.

Jillian sent a separate text message to Hayes only.

I spoke to the lab at Emerald Ridge Hospital and they can do DNA testing today and be discreet with the results. Obviously, you can have it done whenever and wherever you want. As far as I'm concerned, you don't need to do it at all. But I wanted to give you an option that even Taffy can't complain about. It's totally up to you.

Hayes switched back to his email account and replied to everyone.

I will have the DNA test conducted at a reputable facility and the results will be sent to the attorneys. They can determine the validity of the test and then read the results at a family meeting.

He put his phone back in his pocket and stretched his arms over his head. "Okay, with that out of the way, I'm ready to focus on you and Mateo this morning."

Flora smiled, then released a soft sigh. "As much as I'd love for you to hang out and focus on us, Regina is going to be here in an hour, and I need to stop by the shop this morning to go over the weekend sales numbers. But I can do some schedule rearranging if you want me to go to the hospital with you for the swab test."

"No, I don't want you guys to have to change anything." He glanced down at Mateo, who was on his tummy and using one elbow to prop himself up and one foot to push himself in a circle. "You're using an awful lot of energy to spin yourself round and round, partner, but you haven't really gotten yourself anywhere."

As soon as Hayes said the words, he realized that he could've been speaking to himself just as easily. Sure, he was making progress on his relationship with his son and Flora, but having to go through this DNA test felt like he was starting all over again, dealing with the fallout after his father's death.

"I think I'll go back to my hotel and shower, then get this DNA thing over with. I need to do something productive so I don't feel like this little guy down here—just spinning my wheels."

She nodded. "Let me know if you need anything."

He gave both Flora and Mateo a kiss goodbye and waved at Mr. Paul on his way to the truck. Her neighbor seemed preoccupied with something on his phone and didn't notice Hayes or the fact that Velvet was making yet another deposit on the Rodriguezes' front lawn.

Hayes sent Jillian a message thanking her for the info

about the hospital and saying that he hoped they could take walk-ins because he'd be heading that way in an hour.

When he arrived at the small waiting room for the lab department, he was surprised to see his half sister sitting in one of the chairs. His first thought was that Taffy had convinced the others that they needed a witness to vouch for Hayes's identity. But his gut told him that she'd shown up to offer him emotional support.

"You didn't have to meet me here in person," he told Jillian.

"I already had an appointment booked before you texted me back," she replied.

He thought she meant that she'd taken the liberty of booking him an appointment, but then a lab tech opened a side door and Shelby exited into the waiting room. "You're up next, Jillian."

"Be right back," she said as she switched places with her sister.

It still hadn't registered to Hayes why they would both be at the lab at the same time, and then Shelby rubbed her very round midsection. He recalled Flora telling him about all the different tests she'd had when she was pregnant with Mateo, including blood work. "Is Jillian pregnant, too?"

Shelby's eyes widened. "Not as far as I know. Why? Did Nick say something to you?"

Nick Slater worked at Fortune and Daughters Ranch, but Hayes's conversations with Jillian's fiancé had mostly been about horses.

When Madeline walked into the waiting room, though, Hayes realized that this couldn't be a coincidence.

"Sorry I'm late," she said. "My mom was parked in front of my condo, probably on her way to knock on my door since I haven't been returning any of her calls or messages. I don't think she saw me leaving, but I drove around a bit to make sure she wasn't following me here. Did the test hurt at all?"

"Nope." Shelby replied. "Just a swab in your mouth. You have to check in over at the counter and show them your ID."

"Wait." Hayes looked back and forth between the two women. "Are you guys *all* here for a DNA test?"

"Of course," Madeline replied. "If you have to get a test, and the missing heir has to get one—assuming we ever find them—then it seemed only fair that all of us prove we're Dad's kids. Have you signed in yet?"

He was glad to have a task to complete so that he didn't drop into the closest seat and stare up at his sisters in disbelief. With wonder...and gratitude. There were too many emotions roiling through his mind and his body; he wasn't sure which one he felt more.

As the person at the counter checked his identification and completed his paperwork, more emotions were added to the mix already brewing inside him. As angry as Hayes wanted to be at his father for putting all of them in to this situation in the first place, he also wanted to thank the man for giving him these three special women who were showing him what it meant to have sisters.

Jillian returned to the waiting room and Madeline went in next. By the time it was his turn, Hayes wanted to ask the lab tech to give him a few more minutes. This could potentially be the last time he was together with these women before finding out that he wasn't related to any of them. If it turned out he wasn't a Fortune, there would no longer be a reason for them to continue treating him as their brother. For them to interact with him at all.

But Hayes was also determined to move forward with his life, and he couldn't do that until this matter got settled once and for all. He followed the lab tech and decided not to look back.

He nearly laughed when he saw the ordinary looking cotton swab that would ultimately determine his fate, but the test was simple enough. The lab tech explained that the results would be sent to the provided address as soon as they were ready. Afterward, Hayes returned to the waiting room and saw the three women huddled together. They turned in his direction and he shrugged. "I guess all that's left to do now is wait."

Jillian glanced at another patient at the check-in desk and said, "Let's go outside and get some fresh air."

The four of them walked together, but nobody said much until they were outside the hospital and standing under a shady tree in the parking lot. Then the women all turned to look at Hayes again. The back of his neck tingled with awareness.

"Is there something you guys need to tell me?" he asked gruffly.

Madeline spoke first. "The first thing I need to tell you is that I had no idea my mother had hired a private investigator. I'd like to think that if I *had* known, I could've put a stop to it. But you've all met my mom. She would've eventually found a way to get what she wanted."

"Don't worry about it," Hayes told her. "I would never blame you for your mother's actions. In fact, her hiring a PI to look into our backgrounds isn't much different than us hiring one to find Dad's mistress, who clearly doesn't want to be found."

"It *is* different, though. Our intent is to share Dad's legacy—my mom's is to be selfish and spiteful."

He lifted a brow, but didn't even have to ask.

Madeline sighed. "After you and Damaris left the conference room yesterday, my mom said that by proving you aren't one of Dad's heirs, there would be more money for the rest of us."

"I had a feeling that was her motivation." Hayes rolled his shoulders to relieve some of the tension building there. "In fact, I guess that's why I was surprised when I saw you guys here today. You all have a lot to gain if my DNA doesn't match, but you're also risking the possibility that yours might not match Dad's either."

"That was a risk we were willing to take." Shelby sucked in her cheeks. "Anyone else thirsty after all that swabbing? I think I need to hit a drive-through and grab a milkshake on my way to meet Cameron for lunch."

They all politely bowed out. Jillian had to return to the hospital for her volunteer shift and Madeline was meeting with Kate Fortune for more birthday party planning. As for Hayes, he was more than relieved that none of them insisted on staying and discussing test result possibilities because the only thing he wanted to do right now was go see Flora and his son.

"Before I forget," Madeline said, "are you still available to go out to see Susannah Simmons with me tomorrow?"

"No problem. Let me know where to meet you. I might be out at Fortune's Gold this afternoon if I can't find somewhere else that will let me take a horse out for a ride."

"I'm sure you'll want to ride a horse with a little more speed," Jillian said as she typed on her phone. "I'm letting Nick know you're coming out to the ranch. He'll get you set up."

When Hayes climbed inside his truck, he let his head fall back against the headrest. At least the sisters weren't trying to avoid him while they waited for the test results. Not only had they shown up this morning in solidarity to support him, they were still acting as though there was no question that he was their brother.

He had just started the engine when his phone rang and his mom's number popped up on the screen. He waited for the vehicle's Bluetooth to switch on and then answered the call. "Hi, Mom."

"Hi. I saw all the emails from this morning and wanted to check in with you and see how you're holding up."

Hayes told her about the sisters showing up at the hospital to get tested, as well. Then he relayed what Taffy had said after they'd left the meeting yesterday.

"I figured that was what she was up to. As much as I detested that smug expression on her face yesterday, the truth is the truth. This situation is my fault, and I take full responsibility for the choices I made. Taffy was simply the messenger."

"She didn't have to take so much delight in delivering her message, though. Or practically salivate at the chance of getting a bigger inheritance."

"Listen, Hayes. You've got enough going on right now and I don't want you to worry about the inheritance or how it might affect your camps. I already told the attorney that if it turns out that you aren't a Fortune, then I'm signing over my share to you."

"No, Mom. You deserve that money for everything that you had to put up with keeping our family together when Dad wasn't there." What Hayes didn't add was that he was still young enough to go out and earn more money. His mother was getting older and, even if she started charging for her art lessons, she'd never be able to make enough to retire. "But we don't need to waste our time and energy worrying about possibilities and scenarios. Let's wait until the test results come in before talking about all of that."

"Fair enough. I'd much rather save my time and energy for meeting my new grandson. Any chance we could speed that up since I'm already in town?"

It was a good reminder of what mattered more to him than his inheritance or Taffy's allegations.

"Let me call Flora and see if I can work something out."

Flora had about five minutes to get Mateo ready before Hayes and his mom showed up at Lone Star Little Ones.

"I don't like the dark gray on him," Sue said, shaking her head at the short-sleeved, button-up shirt. "He looks like a little storm cloud."

"What if I add this plaid bowtie for a pop of color?"

"Then he'll look like a little storm cloud on his way to an Easter egg hunt. Why does he need to be so dressed up anyway?"

"I want him to make a good impression when he meets

his grandmother for the first time." Flora hadn't exactly come out and told Sue that Hayes was Mateo's father. But, like Regina, she'd figured it out on her own. Or with the help of the other customers at The Style Lounge. Unlike Regina, though, Sue didn't have a direct line of communication to tell Flora's parents.

"Honey, Mateo's grandma isn't going to give a flying fig what this baby has on." Sue started unbuttoning the stiff formal shirt. "And if she does, then you might as well find out now so you can eliminate that type of negativity from the start. Now hand me that blue T-shirt with the silver star decal on the front."

Flora knew the older woman was right, but it didn't make her any less nervous about meeting his mother. Especially under the circumstances.

Sleeping together last night didn't mean she and Hayes were officially a couple. It just meant that they were extremely compatible in bed. Which she'd already known. What Flora didn't know was how all of the changing dynamics happening outside of their relationship would affect them.

As soon as Sue finished swapping outfits, Bettina came into the storeroom and dropped her backpack on the office chair. "Matty's outfit is a total vibe, Miss R."

"A good vibe?" Flora asked, wishing she didn't need validation from two opposite generations. Especially since children's fashion was supposed to be her area of expertise.

"Like *there's a new sheriff in town* vibes."

Flora wasn't sure that was the look she was going for, but she didn't have time for another wardrobe change. When Hayes had called earlier and asked if he could stop by the store with his mom, Flora wasn't sure what would draw less attention to what should be a private moment—a walk in the public park or a chatty high school junior who was hired to help with inventory and deliveries but had somehow appointed herself the content creator for the Lone Star Little Ones social media pages.

Bettina went out to the front of the store then immediately came back and loudly announced, "Hey, Miss R, that snack in the black cowboy hat is here. Hashtag Zaddy."

Flora closed her eyes and counted to three, wishing she had suggested meeting them in the public park. Then she heard the unmistakable sound of the high school marching band across the street and was glad she wasn't outside witnessing yet another promposal.

She took Mateo from Sue and pasted a smile on her face as she left the storeroom.

"No, Mom, a high schooler will hire the band to play a song so they can ask their date to the prom," Hayes explained to the well-dressed woman beside him. "Flora said it's not just a Emerald Ridge thing."

"It's totes romantic," Bettina added from behind the display window as she used her phone to record whatever was happening across the street. "Unless the other person says no. Then it's supes tragic."

Mateo was halfway out of Flora's arms and lunging for Hayes as soon as he heard his father's voice. As usual, Hayes easily lifted the baby into the air and Mateo wasted no time yanking the Stetson off his dad's head.

What *wasn't* usual was the way Hayes dipped his head and gave Flora a quick kiss hello. Her eyelashes fluttered and her cheeks went warm, but she tried to pretend like she'd totally been expecting him to be affectionate in front of his mother. Was this their new normal?

"Mom, this is Flora Rodriguez, and this little deputy with the sheriff's badge on his shirt is Mateo. Flora, this is my mom, Damaris Fortune."

"You are just as perfect as can be," Damaris said to her grandson, the wonder and excitement glowing in her eyes as she clasped her hands in front of her. Her auburn hair was sleek and sophisticated, her jewelry expensive and tasteful, and her clothes had been tailored to fit her perfectly. Flora wouldn't have guessed it was the same woman wearing a Bob Ross T-shirt during the video call a few days ago if she hadn't caught a glimpse of green paint on one of the gold bangle bracelets when Damaris extended a hand in her direction. "Please call me Gigi."

"Mom, you can expect a grown woman to call you by a random nickname you picked out."

"I read that if everyone uses the same name for a person, then that makes it easier for the baby to learn it."

"Hi, Gigi." Bettina waved on her way back to the sales counter. "My grandma used to be a Gigi, but my three-year-old cousin started calling her Greg and now we all do. But she also kinda looks like a Greg."

Flora tilted her head and asked, "How can someone look like a Greg?"

"I don't know how to explain it. She just does. But you definitely look like a Gigi, Gigi."

"Thank you." Damaris smiled as though it was the nicest compliment she'd ever received.

"Mom, do you want to see how close Mateo is to crawling?" Hayes looked at Flora. "Do you mind if we take him over to the play area in the corner?"

"Of course not. That's what it's there for." She had found that parents with smaller children were likely to spend more time shopping in her store when there was something to keep their kids entertained. The area in this shop was smaller than the one in her Houston store, but the yellow area rug customized with the same silhouette in her logo was surrounded by a wooden train table, a basket of display toys and a comfortable rocking chair that nursing mothers appreciated.

Damaris surprised Flora by kicking off her high heels and sitting down on the carpet in her black slacks and silk top. Hayes lowered himself to the opposite corner and sat Mateo between them.

Flora didn't want it to look like she was trying to insert herself into a precious family moment. But there also weren't any customers milling around right now. With Sue prepping gift baskets in the storeroom and Bettina scrolling on her phone behind the register, it would've seemed like Flora was trying to avoid them.

Hayes must have been able to sense her indecision and said, "Flora, I was telling my mom about you craving blueberries when you were pregnant. She said she had the same cravings when she was carrying me."

"It's true." His mother nodded but was completely focused on watching Mateo rock back and forth on his hands and knees. "I can't believe how much he reminds me of Hayes at that age. His little mouth turned up in the corners like that? Oh, my. That smirk used to get me every time."

"I know exactly what you mean," Flora replied with a smile. She didn't add that Hayes's mouth still did that, which was why she lost all good sense when it was aimed in her direction.

Damaris asked questions about Mateo and all of his milestones. At one point, she even lowered herself to her side so she could be on eye level with her grandson. Pride blossomed inside Flora's chest as she watched Mateo's grandmother become more and more smitten by him. Yet there was also a kernel of guilt mixed in with the pride. Flora might've been able to argue that she'd been protecting herself and her son by not telling Hayes about her pregnancy. But her decision had also deprived Damaris of getting to be a grandmother. Or rather a *Gigi.*

A customer came in with three kids under the age of five. The mom told Bettina that she was looking for coordinating outfits for a family photo shoot. A couple of minutes later, the customer's sister arrived with another four children and chaos soon erupted in the store.

The play corner was quickly overrun by youngsters, and Hayes scooped up Mateo just before a rubber duckie came flying in his direction. Sue and Bettina were trying to help with the outfit coordinating, but when a sister-in-law arrived with two more kids who needed to match the rest of the family for the upcoming photo shoot, Flora had to excuse herself so that she could help her staff.

"Since it looks like an all-hands-on-deck type of situation here," Hayes said as he dodged two preschoolers using empty clothes hangers for their sword fight, "do you want me to take Mateo with me?"

"Back to the hotel?" Flora asked as she caught a narrow display rack of clothes that was no match for the stroller obstacle course one of the bigger kids had started.

"Only so I can drop off my mom. I was going to stop

by the Fortune and Daughters Ranch after that. Then we can meet back at the house when you're done."

"Has anyone seen Snowball?" a young girl yelled over the noise. "His cage door is open, and I can't find him anywhere!"

"I *told* you to leave your pet rat in the car," one of the moms scolded, and Flora tried not to shudder.

"It's going to be a while before I can get out of here," she whispered to Hayes.

"Then I'll grab the diaper bag on my way out," he said before dropping a kiss on her lips. Mateo giggled in delight.

It wasn't until the store had completely emptied out two hours later that Flora caught a glimpse of her hair in the fitting room mirror. She nearly shrieked.

"Did you find Snowball?" Bettina asked, reminding Flora that a pet rat was still on the loose in the store.

"Nope." Sighing, Flora gestured to the clip that had turned sideways on her scalp and had pointy chunks of hair sticking up in all directions. "Has my hair been like this all afternoon?"

"Yeah."

"Why didn't you or Sue tell me?"

"I thought that was the look you were going for." Bettina shrugged. "Mateo was dressed like a sheriff and you were the escapee he was hauling back to the insane asylum. I mean your white shirt with those long bell sleeves definitely gives off straitjacket vibes, Miss R."

Flora immediately unclipped her hair and rolled up her sleeves. Although the first impression had already been made, hopefully, Damaris was able to see past her grandson's mother looking like a raving madwoman.

She pulled out her phone and texted Hayes to let him know she was leaving the shop soon.

He replied:

We're still at the ranch. Mateo loves the horses. I might need to get him one for his first birthday.

Flora's stomach dropped and she couldn't unsee the image of her brother's lifeless body in the middle of the rodeo arena. There was a country song warning mothers not to let their babies grow up to be cowboys. She felt every verse of that song as she quickly drove to the Fortune and Daughters Ranch.

# Chapter Eleven

Flora scolded herself for overreacting when she pulled up to the stables at the ranch and saw Mateo perfectly safe in his daddy's arms, gently petting the muzzle of a horse. It wasn't like her child was riding around the corral, earning his first pair of spurs.

Hayes had made a good point about Flora's business logo the other day. In her mind, though, there was a distinct difference between riding a horse and being bucked off one. After all, she couldn't very well raise her son in Texas and expect him to never climb into a saddle.

Flora actually liked horses and wouldn't be against living on a ranch as beautiful as this one. But she also knew her limited skill level when it came to animals that outweighed her by over a thousand pounds.

As she walked up, Mateo saw her and kicked his feet in excitement, the same way he did whenever he saw his dad. Or bananas. Hayes kissed her again, then introduced her to Nick, Jillian's fiancé, and Nick's young niece, Mandy.

"I was telling Hayes that we could get him and Mateo up on a horse this afternoon," Nick said. "But he wanted to run it by you first."

Flora appreciated Hayes anticipating that she might not

be comfortable with the idea of her baby going for a ride. And she wasn't. But she also had to appreciate the fact that horses were a huge part of Hayes's life. Of course, he would want to share that part of himself with his son.

"So you'd be on the horse with him?" She knew the question sounded silly before she asked it. Technically, Mateo could sit up by himself, but his balance wasn't always the best. She didn't trust him alone on a sofa, let alone on a horse.

"Yes. I promise that I'd never do anything that would endanger our son."

Mandy said, "King is real nice."

"My niece is right," Nick added. "King likes kids. In fact, Mandy rides him by herself all the time."

How could Flora possibly argue with the reassurance of a confident preschooler and her doting uncle? She couldn't.

"Okay." Flora tried not to take off running back to the car when Hayes handed Mateo to her. They all walked into the corral, and she had to admit that it did make her feel better to see that Mandy wasn't the least bit afraid of King. Hayes hoisted himself into the saddle and Flora tried not to stare at his muscular legs outlined under his jeans or think about the way they'd been tangled with hers in the sheets last night.

"I'm going to do a lap around the corral to get King accustomed to me. When I come back, you can lift Mateo up to me."

"But how will you hold him and hold the reins at the same time?" she asked, trying not to sound as nervous as she felt.

"The same way I would hold him and cook spaghetti. Trust me, Flora."

Last night, he'd proved himself both strong and agile as he'd lifted her into different positions and, later, easily carried her into the bedroom. The memory, along with a sudden surge of desire for him, almost made her forget about how the spaghetti debacle went.

He did a full lap and even though Mateo was reaching up toward his dad, Flora was still hesitant to hand off her baby just yet. He must've sensed her lingering concern because he slowly did another lap. Leaving Mandy with a few other ranch employees who were now watching, Nick walked along the side of King.

Knowing that another trained cowboy would be right there in case something went wrong helped Flora push aside her fears. This time, when Hayes stopped in front of her, she lifted her excited son into arms that she knew were more than capable.

As soon as Mateo was sitting in the saddle in front of his dad, all of Flora's worries faded into the background as she watched Hayes's skill and the expression of pure joy on her baby's face.

Needing to remember this moment forever, Flora pulled out her phone and took several pictures. Seeing her son's smile made her recall how happy Manny had always been around horses. Her brother would want his nephew to experience that same happiness on a ranch. Someday, Mateo might decide to follow his late uncle's and his father's career path. But Flora wasn't going to worry about someday. She could only think about today.

That evening, after eating the beef stroganoff Regina had left in the oven for them, Hayes was putting Mateo down for bed and Flora realized that it was taking much longer than normal. She'd been eager to hear about the DNA test this morning, but they hadn't had a moment alone so far today.

She peeked into the dimly lit nursery and saw Mateo fast asleep in his father's arms. Hayes sat in the glider, rocking gently as he stared down at his son. When he noticed her at the doorway, he eased himself up and laid Mateo in the crib.

"He fell asleep a while ago," Hayes said quietly when he stepped out of the room. "But I wasn't ready to let go of him yet."

"Some days are like that," Flora murmured back.

"Would you mind if I hopped in the shower?" he asked.

She glanced down at his jeans and button-up shirt. They weren't overly dirty considering he'd spent some time in the stables today. But she doubted anyone would want to put them back on after a shower. Unless he was planning to head directly to her bed afterward, in which case he didn't even need to wear a towel…

But she didn't want to assume he was planning to stay over again. "Of course you can use the shower. I can check my brother Sebastian's room to see if there are any clean clothes that might fit you."

Hayes scrunched his nose in the most adorable way. "No thanks. I brought my own."

Flora looked around the living room. "Where?"

"I have a bag in the truck." There was that charming smirk his mom had mentioned today. "When Mateo and I dropped off my mom at the hotel, I figured I'd grab a few things just in case. By the way, the maître d' at Cucina saw us on our way out and let me know that they have high chairs if we ever want to come in for an early dinner."

Unlike her, he seemed to have no problem assuming there'd be another sleepover tonight.

When he returned with his stuff a minute later, Flora was half tempted to get into the shower with him. But it wasn't quite as big as the one they'd shared in her suite eighteen months ago. She left him a towel and went to get a bottle of wine. He'd had a beer earlier with his dinner—Mateo was starting to get adjusted to everyone eating together and did exceptionally well when French fries were involved—so she grabbed the rest of the six-pack to put in the minifridge of the kitchenette she rarely used.

Hayes emerged from the bathroom wearing sweatpants and a navy-blue T-shirt with the Saddle Up logo on the chest. He saw the beer on the table beside her glass of wine and said, "You are so good at reading my mind."

"Well, it's been a long day."

He collapsed next to her on the sofa and tilted the bottle to his lips. "You can say that again."

"Did everything go okay at the hospital?" she asked, trying not to sound nosy.

"Oh, right. I didn't get a chance to tell you yet. Shelby, Jillian and Madeline were all at the hospital, too. I've only known them a couple of months and I might not even be their brother, yet they were there to not only support me, but to show their solidarity by getting tested, as well. That's why I ended up taking Mateo out to Fortune and Daughters Ranch. Jillian had already told Nick I'd be coming by to see their horses."

"That's pretty commendable of them to show up for

you like that," she smiled. "I bet Madeline's mom isn't going to like her daughter undermining her like that."

"Probably not. But Taffy needs to get used to things not always going her way."

After taking a few sips of merlot, Flora looked at him over the rim of her glass, one brow slightly raised. "What about your brother? Did he take a DNA test, too?"

"You know what? I didn't even have time to call him today to discuss it. Not that I would ask him outright. I don't want him feeling like he has to prove anything to anyone." He sighed, then set his beer bottle aside and turned toward her. "Up until now, he's kept himself pretty removed from the situation. I don't want to do or say anything that might risk alienating him more. If it ends up that I'm not a Fortune after all, then the sisters are really going to need him to help fulfill the terms of the will."

He gave a small shake of his head. "Enough about my family. Tell me about *your* day."

"Well, you had a front-row ticket to how my day went. I hope you told you mom that my store—and my hair—isn't usually that chaotic."

"I loved your eighties' punk rock hair." Hayes chuckled, lifting his bottle for another long drink. "Did they ever find Snowball?"

"No." Flora shuddered again. "Snowball's owner and her mom are going to come tomorrow before the store opens. They think the rat didn't want to come out because of all the people and noise, so they're hoping a quiet evening and a hunk of cheese will help lure Snowball back into its cage."

"My mom liked you, by the way. And I think you could see that she was absolutely enamored by Mateo."

Flora appreciated the reassurance. "Even though he couldn't say Gigi?"

Hayes chuckled again and Flora knew that she was becoming way too fond of the sound. But something told her that he was becoming equally fond of relaxing with her after a long day.

"She'd probably have no problem answering to Greg, if that's what he wanted to call her." He yawned, then looked at his watch before letting his hand drop to her thigh. "I have no idea why I'm so tired. It's not that late."

"Well, you've had an emotional day. And…uh…we didn't get a lot of sleep last night."

He smiled while his hand inched higher on her leg.

"Hold that thought." She returned his smile. "I need to hop in the shower first."

He yawned again. "In that case, I'll wait for you in there."

Hayes jerked his chin toward her bedroom, and Flora, who'd perfected the art of the quick shower after she'd become a mom, tried to beat her personal record. But she hadn't been quick enough. By the time she'd slathered herself with three different types of face and body creams and slipped into something a little sexier than the old T-shirt and faded pajama shorts she normally wore to bed, Hayes was already under the covers and sound asleep.

It should scare her how easily she could picture him there every night. But she was too exhausted to give it any more thought.

Hayes woke up with Flora in his arms and an uncomfortably stiff reminder that he'd fallen asleep last night before she'd come to bed. She pressed her backside closer to him and he began to nuzzle her neck, thinking he'd remedy things this morning.

Unfortunately, before Flora had fully stirred awake, the sound of a lawnmower came from the hallway. No. That wasn't a lawnmower. It was a *vacuum cleaner*. And it was getting closer.

He kissed Flora's temple and whispered her name. Her soft moan didn't help things below his waist.

"Flora," he said a little louder, "I think your house cleaner is here."

"Oh, no," she said, bolting up from the bed. "Is your truck parked out front?"

"It's exactly where I usually park it. Why? I thought you already told her about me."

"I told her that you were Mateo's father and would be visiting him more often. But I also said that things were strictly platonic with us." The way Flora's eyes kept darting toward the door that separated her suite from the hallway, though, made Hayes think that there was something worse than the cleaning lady finding out that he'd spent the night.

"And what did you tell your family?"

"About what?" She yanked the silky—and very small—piece of fabric she'd been sleeping in over her head. Before he could fully appreciate the soft curves of her breasts, though, she was tugging on a Rice University sweatshirt.

"Did you tell your family about me, Flora?"

"Sort of."

*"Sort of?"* His head dropped heavily on the pillow

and he squeezed his eyes shut. “I'm seriously done with all the secrets.”

“I didn't tell them directly, but I'm pretty sure Regina did. Or she will once she realizes that you're sleeping in my bed.”

“Flora, we've been kissing all over town the past few days. Don't you think someone else has brought it up to them?”

“This is a vacation home for them, Hayes. They only know a handful of people. Their business and their lives are in Houston. Or mostly in Houston.” Flora barely pulled the waistband of her yoga pants into place when the door to the suite opened. “Good morning, Regina. You don't need to vacuum in here. I'll be right out.”

“We don't need to pretend there isn't a man in your bed, young lady,” a woman's voice called out. “I already saw his truck outside. Mr. Paul said he's been here all night.”

Hayes wasn't about to hide under the covers. Luckily, he had fallen asleep in his sweatpants so, when he stood up, he was partially clothed. “Hello, ma'am, I'm Hayes Fortune. I really enjoyed your enchiladas last week. And the stroganoff last night.”

Apparently he'd said the right thing because Regina beamed and then stood by the vacuum, asking him about some of his favorite dishes.

Flora cleared her throat. “Regina, what are you doing here on a Tuesday?”

“Oh, your parents called me and said their plane is arriving this afternoon. Your mom wanted me to get things ready for them.”

"What a wonderful surprise." Flora's smile certainly didn't match the panic in her eyes.

Hayes would've laughed at the uncomfortable predicament she'd gotten herself into if he wasn't slightly offended by the realization that she was keeping their relationship a secret from the people she loved most. Just like his mom had kept her affair a secret.

Mateo saved the awkward moment, though, by waking up just then.

"I'll get him," Regina said, abandoning the vacuum in the middle of the room. "You two get dressed and I'll make breakfast."

"Sorry about that," Flora said when they were alone.

"Are you apologizing for the unexpected wake-up call or for not telling your parents that we've been seeing each other? Because there's no need to apologize for Regina doing her job."

"But there *is* a need for me to say sorry about keeping my private life private?"

Hayes ran his hand over the stubble along his jawline. "A year ago, I wouldn't have thought twice about how you explained our relationship to your parents. But after all the revelations about my dad, finding out I had a child, and now this whole DNA test situation—I'm just done with the bombshells."

"I never considered you to be secret." Flora crossed her arms in front of her chest. "But I also know how my parents are, and I didn't want them to get any unrealistic expectations."

"*Unrealistic expectations* about me being the father of their grandchild?"

"No, about us as a couple."

Now he was the one crossing his arms defensively. “You think I don't have those same expectations?”

“I think that everything is happening so fast and there's so many outside variables influencing your emotions right now. How do I know that being with me isn't a substitute for something else you lost? When the dust finally settles with all of your family stuff, you might feel differently.”

“You're doing it again.”

“Doing *what* again?” she huffed.

“The same thing you did after our first weekend together. You didn't want to see me again because you thought I would choose the rodeo over you. Then, when you found out you were pregnant, you didn't tell me about Mateo because you thought I wouldn't want to be his father. Now you want to manage everyone's expectations because you think that I'm eventually going to leave.”

“Is it wrong for me to try and protect myself?”

“The problem is that you're protecting yourself from your own predictions, not from me. Why do you get to be the only one who can decide how I'm going to feel and how I'm going to react to things? Don't I get a choice about how I want to feel?”

“How do you want to feel, Hayes?”

“I want to feel like someone's not going to come and pull the rug out from under me again.” He shoved his hand through his hair in frustration. “I'm all in on this, Flora. I want to be here every day for Mateo, and for you. But you have to be all in on us, too. Are you?”

Before she could answer, his phone rang on the bedside table where he'd left it.

When he made no move to reach it, she said, "Shouldn't you take that?"

"It's probably Madeline. I told her I'd run an errand with her this morning. I can call her back. This conversation is important, Flora."

"Everything is important, Hayes. Eighteen months ago when we met, neither one of us had a care in the world other than our jobs. Of course I want to be all in with you. But with so many variables in our lives right now, how do either of us know what being all in entails?"

She'd said *our* lives, but really, they both knew that she meant *his* life. It was his family drama that had him spinning in circles.

"I don't have the slightest clue," he admitted. Hell, he didn't even know who he was if it turned out that he wasn't a Fortune after all. He was already thinking about what it would be like once he had to extricate himself from his sister's lives. It made his stomach turn to think of having to lose Flora, too.

"Then the best we can do is take each change, each bombshell, one day at a time. And today, I need to deal with the bombshell of explaining to my parents that currently I'm hooking up with a former rodeo cowboy, who also happens to be the father of child."

Hayes cringed. "Maybe you could describe our situation a little more…"

She lifted her brows expectantly, but he let the suggestion hang in the air since this was one problem that didn't involve people with the same last name as him.

"Right." He nodded. "I'll just call Madeline back and see where she wants to meet."

* * *

"Are you sure this Susannah Simmons person lives here?" Hayes asked Madeline as they parked in front of a tightly closed gate with several no-trespassing signs.

"This is the address Kate Fortune gave me. Although, it doesn't look like the lux retreat I was expecting." She opened her passenger door. "I don't see any kind of intercom system out here. Maybe we can just let ourselves in."

Hayes followed her to the thick wooden gate that, from the road, looked like a soft breeze could knock it over. He was surprised to see that it was actually quite sturdy and firmly locked.

It was also apparently guarded by a loud dog with a ferocious bark. Madeline jumped back at the first woof and Hayes scanned the fence line to make sure there weren't any holes that a determined dog could get through. That's when he saw the state-of-the-art surveillance camera mounted to one of the fence posts. It was directed right at Hayes and Madeline.

"I'm pretty sure that whoever lives here, doesn't like having company show up unannounced."

"Then they should've returned my call," Madeline retorted, pushing on different areas of the gate as if there were some hidden lever that would open it.

"I'd suggest you write a letter and slip it under the gate, but that snarling dog on the other side might eat it."

A black-and-white cruiser turned off the road and parked behind the truck. Hayes glanced back up at the video camera, thinking that whoever had called law enforcement was important enough to get a fast response time, considering the ranch was in a remote location.

Two officers exited the vehicle. The younger one kept

his hand close to his gun belt while the middle-aged one walked as though he was out for a casual stroll.

"Did you folks notice the no-trespassing signs?" The question came from the younger cop, who barely looked old enough to shave.

"It's kind of hard not to notice them, Rook," the other officer told his partner, who was clearly still in training.

"We aren't trespassing," Madeline said. "I'm just trying to get in touch with the owner."

"It's private property," the younger one reminded them, then flinched when the dog started barking again. He recovered quickly, though. "So, if you're not invited guests, then you're both trespassing."

"We haven't gone inside the gate, though." Madeline smiled brightly and Hayes realized that his sister had the situation under control.

"But you touched the gate. And the gate *is* private property." Rookie moved his hand to the pouch on his belt that held the handcuffs.

Hayes's shoulders went back as he was about to interject when the training officer took a few steps closer and shook his head at the trainee.

"Nobody is under arrest. We just stopped by to issue a warning."

"Right." The younger one thankfully left his handcuffs in place. "And to advise you to leave the premises immediately."

"Fine," Madeline sighed. "We'll leave."

"Before you take off, though…" The middle-aged officer pulled a small notebook out of his chest pocket. "Would you mind me asking for an autograph, Mr. Fortune? My son's been a big fan ever since I took the family to Frontier Days in Cheyenne and we saw you go three rounds on Widowmaker."

It had been a while since someone had recognized Hayes outside of the rodeo arena, he'd almost forgotten that aspect of his past life.

"No problem," he said, making sure the notepad he was signing wasn't actually a ticket citing him for trespassing.

"If you want, I can get a picture of you guys," Madeline offered. No wonder she was such a successful party planner—she knew how to keep everyone happy. Even the trainee cop who'd been ready to throw the book at them was handing over his phone so she could snap a photo with his camera, too.

As they drove off, Hayes told her as much.

"Thanks," she replied. "When that younger officer went for his handcuffs, all I could think was that I'd have to send Kate Fortune an invoice charging her for bail money."

"After you told the other cop that his son might be interested in attending my rodeo camp for free, I wouldn't be surprised if they offered to give Susannah Simmons a police escort to her great-great-great-aunt's birthday party."

When Madeline had mentioned Saddle Up, Hayes heard Flora's words from this morning replay in his head. There was always something coming up that required him to put everything else in his life on the back burner. Sure, he had a capable board of directors running the nonprofit for him, but as his social media director liked to remind him, one of the biggest draws to the camps was name recognition. As much as he preferred staying out of the limelight, donors wanted to mingle at fundraisers with him and campers wanted to meet him. He needed to figure out a better way of prioritizing.

Obviously, his son was now at the top of his list of priorities, which meant Flora was right up there, as well. But all of his siblings were still dealing with their personal lives while all the Archibald drama was unfolding. Hell, even Madeline was finding time to deal with her obnoxious mother while simultaneously planning a huge hundredth birthday party for a woman who sent her out on pointless quests like this one.

Maybe Flora was right. Maybe Hayes did have too much stuff going on in his life. He'd asked her point-blank this morning if she was all in and, as much as his heart had sagged in relief when she admitted she was, his brain also heard everything else she'd said. And everything she didn't say. His entire career had trained him to expect the unexpected, to take one ride, one go-round at a time. In the back of his mind, however, there was still the nagging reminder that his father had been so preoccupied juggling multiple obligations at the same time, the man hadn't been able to keep everyone happy. To keep everyone a priority. Hayes never wanted Mateo or Flora to feel that way.

As he was contemplating the best way to prove himself to them, both his phone and Madeline's phone rang at the same time. His dash screen showed the caller right as she said, "It's the attorneys…the DNA results must be in."

## *Chapter Twelve*

Flora checked her phone several times to make sure she hadn't missed a message from Hayes. Usually by this time of day, he'd write her a quick message asking about Mateo's nap or sending her a link to a picture or an article he'd seen that reminded him of her or their son. Sometimes it was something as simple as the online menu for a restaurant asking for her takeout order.

After the way they'd left things this morning, though, she wouldn't be surprised if she didn't hear from him for a while.

She knew he hadn't liked hearing what she'd had to say, but the truth was that Mateo needed consistency. And right now, there wasn't much in Hayes's life that was consistent. That didn't mean that they wouldn't get there eventually, but both of them needed to face the reality that not everything was going to be as easy at it had been that first weekend they'd met.

Her phone rang and Flora tried to sound cheerful after she saw that it wasn't him calling. "Hi, Mom."

"Hi, honey. Your dad is on speaker with me. We just landed in New York for a quick layover. Our flight to Dallas boards in an hour—" The airport loudspeaker interrupted with a reminder to not leave bags unattended but it didn't stop her mom from talking, it only made Elena Rodriguez speak louder. "We should be driving into Emerald Ridge in time for dinner."

"A late dinner." Omar didn't correct his wife very often, but when he did, it was usually about food.

"Not too late, though," her mom added. "In case you want to invite your friend over to eat with us."

"My friend?" Flora asked, even though she knew full well who her mother was talking about.

"Mateo's father. Regina said he's related to that Fortune family with the dad who was married to three different women."

So much for thinking that her parents weren't up to date on the Emerald Ridge gossip.

"Does your friend work for Fortune Air?" her dad asked. "Because I've been a platinum mileage member for over twenty years now and I don't understand why they'd change the snack mix in the VIP lounge. They used to have those honey-roasted peanuts, Elena, remember? And now it's those unsalted almonds that don't—"

"Hayes doesn't work for Fortune Air, Dad," Flora interrupted before her father began describing his all-time favorite lounge snack. "Mom, tonight might not be the best time to meet him."

"Then we can meet him tomorrow."

"Biscuits and gravy from the Emerald Ridge Café is the perfect cure for jet lag," Omar said. "Hayes can join us for breakfast."

Flora looked at the ceiling and prayed for patience before saying, "Let's not rush into any plans just yet."

"Who's rushing into anything?" her mom asked.

"You've known him for eighteen months already. Is having one brunch with him too much to ask?"

Flora might have met Hayes eighteen months ago, but she hadn't really known him until recently.

Omar, though, was already making his own correction. "Technically, it would be breakfast unless we went to Captain's. They do a nice seafood brunch."

"No breakfast or brunch, okay? Hayes has a lot going on at the moment," she told her parents, working to keep her tone even as she clung to the last thread of her patience. "I'm not sure what all you've heard about his dad passing away…"

"Only that there was more than one Mrs. Archibald Fortune as a registered guest at the hotel when they did the will reading. Omar, if I ever find out that you have other wives, you're going to meet the business end of my pickleball racket."

"Physical violence doesn't suit you, *mi amor*," her father said to his normally even-tempered wife. "Besides, I don't have time for another wife. I go everywhere with you. We even carpool to the office together."

Flora heard the sound of kissing in the background and wondered how long it would be before Mateo stopped giggling every time his own parents kissed and started rolling his eyes the same way she did after twenty-eight years of having to wait for her parents to finish being affectionate with each other.

The airport loudspeaker came on again and must've reminded the Rodriguezes that their daughter was still on speakerphone.

"We expect to meet him while we're in town, Flora."

Had her mom not heard what Flora had said earlier?

"We will see," she replied, knowing that she couldn't put off the inevitable. "Like I said, he has a lot going on right now. Everything is complicated and emotionally fragile right now. Adding my family to the mix this soon might scare Hayes away."

Her father's tone was no longer lighthearted. "If a man gets scared away so easily, *mija*, then he's no man at all."

Great. Now she'd gone and made Hayes sound like the type of person who couldn't handle something as simple as meeting her parents. Maybe he was right and that she tried to control situations by predicting how people would feel and react. Right now, her record on what she thought would happen compared to what actually happened was zero and three.

At this point, Flora wouldn't even bet on herself.

She had no more than hung up with her parents when her phone rang again. This time it *was* Hayes.

"Hi," she said eagerly, not even pretending to sound busy.

"Hey. We didn't talk about dinner before I left, but I was thinking… If you need time to talk to your parents first, then I can skip tonight with Mateo."

It was the first time he hadn't insisted on being with them in the evenings and a flicker of apprehension made her fingers tense as she held the phone.

"Well, my parents probably won't be here until after Mateo goes to bed anyway. So, if you still want to come over for the bedtime routine, you can. And if you want to stay later and meet them when they arrive, that's up to you."

Hayes released a deep breath, and she could imagine the way his head would be tilted back, his lips opening slightly as he exhaled. "I would like to do both. But I might not make the best impression on them tonight. The attorneys were able to put a rush on the DNA test results and they've called a meeting tomorrow morning to go over them."

"Wow, that was fast," she said. As nerve-racking as it'd be to wait a whole week for DNA results, it must be just as intense knowing that as soon as tomorrow morning, his whole world might change. Yet again. "How are you feeling about finding out?"

"The same way I used to feel before we drew horses to see which one I'd be riding. Except multiply that by a hundred."

"Really? The draw worried you more than trying to climb on the back of an angry horse?"

"Being inside the chute was the easy part because, by then, I'd already committed to staying on that horse no matter what. That was my job, and I knew how to do it. But those moments before the draw when everything is undecided? It's the not knowing that I don't like."

Flora had a feeling his analogy wasn't limited to the unknown results of the DNA test. Once Hayes had seen Mateo, he had jumped right into fatherhood and was holding on to the reins for all he was worth.

Again, she wanted to apologize for not telling him about the pregnancy. But the only way for them to move forward was by not repeating the same mistakes. By not assuming she knew his feelings better than he knew himself.

"Luckily, I have something to help distract me from spending the entire night worrying about some numbers on a piece of paper." It was easy to assume Hayes was talking about her and Mateo being a distraction since that had been suggested this morning. So, she was surprised when he said, "Plus, I need to go over a bunch of budget stuff that the Saddle Up board of directors sent me and be ready to make an offer on a Montana property for our next ranch location."

*Montana property* sounded a lot farther away than buying a spread in Emerald Ridge. But Hayes had always been up front about enjoying a career that allowed him to be on the road. He also had a great exit strategy in place in the event he wanted one.

Tonight, though, she wasn't going to make any more predictions. Just like Mateo had adapted to the consistency of having Hayes putting him to bed every night, she and her son would have to learn to adapt to whatever happened next.

Getting through one night without him should be a breeze after doing it on her own for so long. Shouldn't it?

Hayes sat by his mother in the conference room he now associated with some of the most painful revelations that changed the trajectory of his life. The only place he possibly despised more than this one had been the hospital room where a doctor had once told him that he might not walk again.

He wished he'd stayed out in the hallway, waiting until the last possible minute before coming in and taking his seat. Now, he had to pretend to be looking at anything other than the faces across from him as the women—he was already training himself not to think of them as his sisters anymore—attempted to ease the tension in the room by talking about anything but what had brought them here today.

Hayes, though, hadn't said a single word. Instead, he cataloged everything he didn't like in this room. He hated the pattern on the carpet. He hated the color of the chairs. He even hated the clock on the wall with the second hand ticking loudly as they waited for the attorneys to arrive. He was trying not to add his father's third wife to the list, but he did allow himself to hate Taffy's pretend, overpriced cowboy boots that wouldn't last a day on a working ranch.

The door opened at ten o'clock on the dot, and his dad's lawyers walked inside. Hayes tried not to blink as the men filed in, but he would never get used to the sight of triplets in business suits.

"Finally," Taffy said from the other end of the conference table.

But the attorneys took their time opening their matching briefcases and pulling out what looked to be duplicate file folders and sealed envelopes.

Huey, Louie or possibly Dewey, cleared his throat. "We will get started as soon as everyone is here."

"This *is* everyone." Taffy made a sweeping gesture of the room. "Or at least everyone who's bothered showing up the last two times."

Hayes knew that if he looked at his mom right then, he'd see the disappointment on her face, so he kept his eyes fixed on the three men at the front of the room. His attention was so focused on figuring out which one was Carlton, he didn't see the door open.

"Sorry I'm late." Penn's voice flooded the room and

their mother gasped. "The runway was a mess at the airfield."

Hayes swiveled in his chair with so much force, it nearly rotated all the way around again. He shot to his feet and asked, "What are you doing here, Penn?"

"I'm guessing the same thing you're all doing here. Although, I don't need a DNA test to tell me that you're my brother. No matter what the results say, nothing is going to change that."

Hayes had never been happier to see his big brother, and pulled him into a hug. Penn returned the embrace and added a few hefty pats to his back.

"If everyone's done with the sickeningly sweet display of brotherly love, can we please find out whether or not Hayes is a Fortune?" Taffy sniped.

One of the attorneys picked up the sealed envelope in front of him and opened it. He cleared his throat and said, "With a 99.7 percent certainty rate, Madeline Fortune is the daughter of Archibald Fortune."

"You mean *Hayes*?" Taffy asked, looking between the attorney and her daughter. "You said Madeline, but it was Hayes who was getting tested."

"We all got tested,." Madeline folded her hands in her lap. "If one of us had to prove they're a Fortune, then all of us should have to prove it."

"Why? I wasn't the one who cheated on Archie."

"Stop causing so much unnecessary drama, Mom. It's getting tiresome and you're starting to sound petty."

"Can we do mine next?" Jillian nodded eagerly toward the two envelopes sitting in front of the second attorney.

In keeping with the practice of Archibald assigning one attorney to each of his families, the result for each offspring was read by their designated attorney. It wasn't a surprise that Jillian's and Shelby's results proved they were also Fortunes, both of them with a 99.7 percent certainty, as well.

There was a slight moment of uncertainty when the third attorney paused before reading Penn's test results. Carlton held the paper at a distance as he squinted. Once he pulled a pair of glasses out of his pocket and placed them on his nose, though, he announced that there was a 99.8 percent certainty that Penn was Archibald's son, as well.

With one envelope left, it was finally time for the moment of truth. Hayes felt his mom's hand slip into his and he squeezed it to reassure her that they would be fine no matter what the results were.

"With a 99.9 percent certainty rate, Hayes Fortune is the son of Archibald—"

Whoops and cheers drowned out the rest and the three attorneys barely managed to get out of the way in time for Shelby, Jillian and Madeline to come running around the table to hug Hayes.

"Let me look at that paper," Taffy demanded.

"Would you please just shut up?" Agatha, of all people, said to her husband's third wife.

Damaris, Hayes's very classy mother didn't bother wiping away the tears from her eyes when she added, "Taffy, you can take that paper and shove it up—"

Hayes pulled his mom into a tight embrace before she could finish that statement. "I am so glad that we can put that behind us now."

"Me, too," Damaris whispered as she squeezed him back.

Jillian cleared her throat. "So...uh... Hayes, do you want to introduce us to our *other* brother?"

"Penn, these are your sisters," Hayes told the newcomer, whose expression suggested he wasn't so sure about not including the word *half* with sisters before being pulled in for group hug.

"So how long will you be in town, Penn?" their mother asked.

"I guess as long as it takes to fulfill the terms of Dad's will." He tugged on his ear after the sisters let out another round of cheers. "I hope this hotel has a bar."

"It does, but we also have plenty of bars in Emerald Ridge," Jillian said. "We'll have you feeling right at home in no time."

Hearing the word *home*, Hayes immediately wanted to call Flora and tell her the news. But he also had his family surrounding him wanting to celebrate. He could slip away to send a quick text, but after not seeing her last night, it felt like something he should tell her in person.

"Anyone up for an early lunch?" Shelby asked.

"I am." Madeline held up her hand. "I was so nervous about today, I skipped breakfast."

"I'll drive," Jillian offered. "I've got the investigator's files in my car and we can get Penn caught up on everything."

Penn's eyes went wide. When he only got Hayes's knowing smirk as reassurance, he said, "I should probably drive my mom."

"I'm going to pass on lunch," Damaris murmured. "This morning is catching up with me and I need some quiet time to clear my head."

Agatha was already walking out of the room with one

of the attorneys and Taffy had completely disappeared, possibly pouting now that she wasn't getting any extra inheritance.

"Penn, why don't you and I walk Mom to her room and then we can meet everyone at the restaurant?"

It didn't take long, though, for him and Penn to give their mom a hug goodbye at the door to her room. When they came back downstairs, the sisters were still in the lobby, talking.

"Slight change of plans," Shelby said to her brothers. "We're going to leave our cars here and walk to Francesca's. It's only a few blocks away."

They were on the opposite side of the street from Lone Star Little Ones and Hayes was tempted to pop his head into the store and give Flora an update. He also wanted to introduce Penn to Mateo. But he wasn't even sure if Flora had gone into work today since her parents' flight had been delayed and he'd been so absorbed in his thoughts about today's meeting, he hadn't thought to ask.

He definitely didn't want to talk about his questioned paternity in front of her folks the very first time he met them. Not that there was ever a good time to bring it up. As soon as lunch was over, he'd call her and hope nothing else would happen to ruin what had the potential to be a perfect day.

Flora was walking toward the window display Sue had just finished when a black Stetson across the street caught her eye. She recognized the three Fortune sisters, but didn't know who the other man was with them. Everyone seemed to be smiling as they talked, so hopefully, the family meeting this morning had gone well.

She hadn't really expected Hayes to contact her right away if he was upset about the DNA results. But it kind of stung that he hadn't shared any potentially good news with her either. What was she expecting, though? A text with the thumbs-up emoji?

She'd given him an earful about all the variables in their lives and figuring out what it entailed. That required patience, something that they didn't seem to have much of whenever they were together. She really needed to be taking her own advice.

And right now, her priority needed to be this shop. She left Sue on the sales floor and went back to the storeroom to pull up the inventory lists for the Houston store and make sure they had the same products in stock for the summer season.

Ninety minutes later, her parents walked in, pushing Mateo in his stroller. She'd appreciated their offer to babysit this morning, and Flora had managed to get quite a bit done without him underfoot. Still, her heart expanded when she saw her son after missing him for a few hours.

"We stopped by to see if you wanted to grab some lunch," her father said.

Flora's stomach nearly growled at the mention of food. "You have no idea how good that sounds."

She grabbed her purse and followed them to the front of the store. "Sue, we're going to get some lunch. Do you want us to bring back anything?"

"Maybe a new employee who can run the cash register for me?" The older woman chuckled but was completely serious.

"I'll see if they have that on the menu," Flora replied,

but the only person who laughed at the joke was her father.

It really was time to hire a few new people. Flora had devoted so much of her energy to opening this shop, she had all but abandoned the Houston store. Besides, once the baby became more mobile, she wouldn't be able to bring him to work as often.

They were halfway down the block when Mateo started babbling and pointing across the street. Her mom was pushing the stroller and her dad was standing immediately to Flora's right, so she couldn't see what had captured the baby's interest until he stepped up onto the sidewalk and was standing in front of them.

"Hey, partner." Hayes squatted until he was eye level with the stroller. "Who do you have with you?"

Mateo answered by taking his father's hat.

Hayes stood to his full height and didn't wait for Flora to make the introductions. "Hello, ma'am, I'm Hayes Fortune." He shook her mom's hand first and then her father's. "Nice to meet you, sir."

"Flora has told us absolutely nothing about you," her mom said with a teasing smile.

"I've told them the basics," Flora insisted. "Regina filled them in on the rest before I had a chance."

"Heard you know your way around horses," her dad said. "But that your taste in chili is questionable."

"Dad!" Flora scolded, but Hayes only laughed. There was a definite lightheartedness around his eyes that was new. She let the hopeful feeling in her chest spread inside of her and smiled.

The man she'd seen with Hayes earlier crossed the

street toward them. "The sisters are heading back to the hotel. I told them we'd catch up with them later."

Hearing someone refer to his Fortune siblings as *the sisters* was another good sign that the family meeting had gone well earlier. Not wanting to ask Hayes in front of her parents, though, Flora lifted her eyebrows, hoping he picked up on her unspoken question.

He smiled and gave her a quick nod, making her shoulders sag with relief. "Mr. and Mrs. Rodriguez, Flora, this is my brother, Penn Fortune."

Flora's brows shot up again. His brother had finally come to Emerald Ridge! Hopefully, that was another positive development.

There was another round of hand-shaking before Hayes added, "And the little partner who likes to steal my hat is your nephew, Mateo."

"You weren't joking about those eyes, man." Penn lowered himself in front of the stroller. "Your daddy sent me pictures, kiddo, but seeing it in person is a whole other level. Nobody needs a DNA test with you."

Flora's father made a sound in the back of his throat and Penn stood up immediately. "No offense, sir. I didn't mean to suggest that your daughter—"

"It's been a big morning for us Fortunes," Hayes interrupted. "We've been throwing around terms like *DNA* and *genetics* and *99.9 percent certainty* for the past couple of hours."

*Ninety-nine point nine?* Flora moved her lips as she silently repeated what he'd just said. Hayes nodded again, his smile even bigger.

"Yeah, who would've thought that the kid who looks the least like our father would end up with the most certainty?" Penn said. Clearly, both Fortunes weren't big on secrets or on keeping family business private. "Although, 99.8 percent ain't too shabby either."

"I understand your father recently passed," Flora's mom said softly. "My condolences."

Both men thanked her, but Flora's father took the opportunity to ask, "Will either of you be taking over Fortune Air?"

"Omar." Flora's mom hissed. "Do you seriously think now is the best time to bring this up?"

"Who else am I supposed to talk to about the snack mix in the VIP lounge, Elena?"

"Oh, I don't know. Any one of the hundreds of employees that work there?"

Hayes was trying to hold back a smile, but Penn pointed his finger and asked, "Are you talking about the salt-free almonds?"

"Yes!" her dad said a bit too loudly. "What I want to know is what was wrong with the honey-roasted peanuts?"

"I think that was a vendor change that somehow got slipped by my dad. I'll look into it." Penn pulled a gold membership-looking card out of his wallet. "In the meantime, next time you travel, I hope you'll be my guest at Fortune Resorts. Our concierge-preferred suites are stocked with the original snack mix."

"Elena, that's the hotel you loved in London." Flora's father happily took the offered card. "I know where I'm taking you for our anniversary."

"We better let you get going," Hayes said to the group, then shifted his gaze to Flora. "Should I call you later about dinner?"

She nodded, slightly excited that he was sticking to the new routine, but also unsure if he was going to kiss her in front of everyone.

Her heart skipped, anticipation curling low in her belly. He took a few steps toward her and Flora reminded herself to stay cool. But before he could pass the stroller, her mom said, “Don’t forget your hat.”

Hayes smiled at Mateo. “He can keep it. I’ve got another one in the truck.”

# *Chapter Thirteen*

Hayes walked back to the hotel with Penn and waited for his brother to check in. After he made several comparisons of this lobby to the lobby at his hotel in Houston.

"Thanks again for showing up this morning," Hayes told him.

"*Thank you* for getting the investigation started and dealing with all the crap while I took my time delaying the inevitable."

Hayes shrugged. "I knew you'd come around eventually."

"At this rate, I'm just glad I made it before the wedding."

"Which one? Shelby's or Jillian's?" As far as Hayes knew, neither of his sisters had set a date yet.

"Yours, man." Penn laughed when Hayes narrowed his eyes in doubt. "I saw the way you were looking at Flora. It's clear your heart is already here in Emerald Ridge. Why waste another eighteen months?"

"Because a lot can change in eighteen months?"

"Yeah, but the way you feel about her, and your son, isn't going to change."

He couldn't stop the wide grin spreading across his face.

"I used to hate it when you were right," he told his big brother.

"Well, you got to be right last week. It's my turn this week." Penn clapped him on the back. "I'm heading up to my room to read the PI file. I'm sure you have more important things to do right now than rehash everything I've missed."

That was certainly an understatement. Hayes left his brother in the lobby and, even though he still needed to return his Realtor's call and review the job applications for the incoming camp counselors this summer, he still needed to process everything that had happened this morning. He headed toward the parking lot, thinking he'd drive out to Fortune and Daughters Ranch and take a long ride. But for some reason, his boots led him in a different direction, and he found himself walking in the park.

He found the same bench he'd sat on when he'd come here with Flora over a week ago. Hayes could hardly believe how much had happened in such a short amount of time. He used to rush through life, leaving one adventure to run headfirst into the next. But now, Hayes took a seat on the bench, wanting time to slow down.

Why hadn't he noticed all the young, happy families in this town before now? Kids playing on the grass with their moms handing out snacks on picnic blankets, toddlers on their father's shoulders, parents walking together, holding hands. When he looked at Flora and Mateo, this was what he envisioned for his future. But what if he fell short of being the kind of father he wanted to be? What if that Fortune DNA of his eventually resulted in him being the same type of dad his father had been?

Then again, Archibald had had three families, plus a mistress, not to mention the multibillion-dollar company he'd been running. Maybe Hayes didn't give his old man enough credit for the amount of time he'd managed to be with them in Houston.

"Hayes?" someone said as they came up from behind the bench. "I almost didn't recognize you without your hat."

"Roth." Hayes stood to shake his distant cousin's hand. "I almost didn't recognize *you* strolling around so comfortably with a toddler on your shoulders."

"I wasn't always this comfortable," Roth replied rather candidly. "In fact, I was hesitant about dating a single mom. But I wouldn't trade becoming Georgie's daddy for the world."

"Found it!" Antonia Leonetti walked up with a small pink sneaker and Hayes noticed her almost-two-year-old was missing a shoe. "Hi, Hayes. I can't believe how many of you Fortunes are showing up for Kate Fortune's birthday."

"My sister Madeline is hoping for a big turnout," Hayes said, not bothering to tell his cousin's fiancée that a hundredth birthday party was actually the last reason why he was in Emerald Ridge. "Penn just got into town this morning so there's more of us popping up all over the place."

They spoke for a few more minutes and Hayes saw someone in the distance wearing a uniform and, suddenly, an idea began to take shape in his head. Hadn't he already proved that he would be a better father than

Archibald? He sure as hell had proved that he was done living in the past and ready to face the next challenge head-on. He didn't need a DNA test to tell him what he already knew about himself. When something felt right, it felt right.

Flora heard the distinctive sound of a trombone and a snare drum before she heard her mother call down the hallway, "Flora, there's someone here for you."

The music grew louder as Flora carried her son to the front door. It sounded like… *No, it couldn't be…*

"Why is the entire high school marching band on my front lawn?" Her dad was in the middle of the porch, holding his barbecue tongs.

"Get out of the way, Omar," her mom said. "I'm trying to record the promposal."

Except it wasn't a promposal.

Hayes stood in front of the band holding a huge sign that said, Will You Marry Me, Flora?

It was a real proposal. And in true Hayes style, he was not making a secret of it.

When the cymbals crashed on the last note of the Taylor Swift song that had been played all over Emerald Ridge, Hayes walked toward her and dropped down on one knee. "Flora, when I met you eighteen months ago, I thought to myself that you were the exact type of woman that I'd want to marry. You're funny and smart and creative. You're the calm to my storm. And you're a helluva good mother. I want to have more babies with you. I want to share all the firsts with you. I can't imagine life being married to anyone but you."

"I can't believe I fell in love with a headstrong cowboy, but here we are." Flora handed Mateo to her dad and threw herself into Hayes's arms. "I love you and can't wait to be your wife. I thought you'd never ask."

"I *knew* he'd ask," her mother said. Flora turned around in time to see her father make a shushing gesture to his wife.

"He called me this afternoon," her dad said. "But I didn't know there'd be a band involved."

Her mother, though, rolled her eyes. Flora immediately knew that wasn't what her mother had meant.

"Mom, is there something you want to share with me and the entire Emerald Ridge High School marching band?" Oh, and Velvet, who was currently sniffing his favorite spot on their grass.

"All I was saying is that as soon as Hayes showed up in town, I told your father that it was only a matter of time."

Hayes had already stood up, his arm still tightly wrapped around her waist. "You guys knew who I was when I first got here? Before I even saw Mateo in Flora's store."

Her dad pretended to pinch Mateo's nose with his barbecue tongs, making the baby laugh. "Let's just say that the Fortunes aren't the only ones who know how to hire private investigators."

"Dad!" Flora said. "Please tell me that you didn't."

"We don't do secrets in this house, *mija*. And your mother got tired of waiting for you to tell us."

"It's true. You know how impatient I get."

Flora turned to apologize to Hayes, but he was bent over, holding his stomach as he laughed harder than she'd ever heard him laugh before.

She waited for him to stop before she asked, "Are you sure you don't want to rethink marrying into this family?"

He answered by pulling a ring box out of his pocket. "You get my family and I get yours. That's the deal."

Mateo made the smacking sound with his lips.

Flora's cheeks ached from smiling. "In that case, your son and I both say yes."

Hayes sealed the agreement with a kiss.

* * * * *